MW00760930

Slave, Brave, and Free

By
Cal Bombay
with Margaret Sharpe

Loyal Publishing
www.loyalpublishing.com

Dedication

This book is dedicated to my son John and my daughter Elaine who listened to this as a spontaneously told story, night after night, as they were put to bed in Africa over thirty years ago. Years later, I began to tell the story again, made up, incident after incident, to my grandchildren, Joshua and Tori. And to my daughter-in-law, Karen, who stuck a Dictaphone in my face as I retold the story, and who typed up the first transcript. And, to my wife Mary who gives me all the encouragement and latitude to sit for hours and write.

I love you all!

- Cal. R. Bombay

To Mike, strong, brave and free.

- Margaret Sharpe

Contents

Chapter 1

Slave

"Get up, slave! I'm gonna whip your heathen hide!"

Jerked from sleep by Mister Payne's shout, Okot scrambled off his straw mattress. Stumbling to his feet, he banged his head as usual on the rough board ceiling of the cabin. The overseer's whip snapped out, quick as a snake striking from the grass. It stung Okot's shoulder like a hot brand, and he felt blood trickling down his back. "I hate you, Payne!" he wanted to scream, but that would only get him a worse whipping. He ground his teeth and kept quiet.

The overseer screamed with rage. He loved to make his slaves snivel and beg for mercy. Okot's silence sent him into a frenzy. "Why, you lazy pig!" he shrieked, "I'll teach you to respect me!" Spit flew from Payne's mouth and hit Okot on the cheek. It smelled sour, like rotting grass after a long rain. Okot wiped it off and Payne saw the disgust on his face. The whip struck out again and again. Payne was half blind with anger and he hit the air as often as he hit Okot. Okot cringed against the wall, breathing hard. The whites of his eyes showed like two full moons in his black face. He held out his long thin arms in front of him as though that would somehow stop the lashing.

Payne was in charge of all thirty slaves on Master Abbot's plantation. He was always finding reasons to punish them, but the whippings were worst in the mornings when his eyes were bleary from a night of drinking whisky. The older slaves told Okot he should learn to cry so that the whipping would be over faster. But Okot couldn't do it.

Here on the Abbot plantation in Virginia he was just a slave boy. But in Africa, before the terrible day when the slave raiders came to his village, he had been the son of a proud Dinka chief. Okot was only eleven, but all his life he had learned from his father how to protect his family's herds of cattle, sheep and goats, and how to protect his younger brothers and sisters from all the dangers in their land. There was danger from lions and hyenas, from leopards and wild dogs. Danger from the crocodiles that lurked under muddy river waters. Danger from the buffalo that charged without warning, goring people and livestock with their sharp thick horns. Danger from the poisonous snakes that hid in the grasslands and trees, and from the scorpions that could kill a strong bull or cow.

Only a year before the slave raiders came, Okot had been bitten by a poisonous cobra. His father showed him how to cut open his skin across the fang marks and suck out the venom. For days he had been sick with fever, and from his bed in the dark, smoky hut he imagined he saw evil spirits fighting for his soul. But he had lived. He was proud of the thick white scar just above his left knee. He would *never* cry because of a white man's beating.

Payne wasn't any taller than Okot. Like all the Dinka people, Okot was long and slender as a crane. But Payne was a great hulk of a man, and he seemed to tower over Okot in the hut. He had a fat, pale face that went beet red when he was angry—which was most of the time—and wet, rubbery lips and sagging skin like a hippopotamus.

Near Okot's village of Nyamlel, the hippos cooled themselves in the heat of the day by sinking their great lumbering bodies in the river Lol. Nothing but their snouts and eyes showed above the water, looking like harmless rocks. And they didn't hurt anyone, as long as you left them alone.

But Payne wasn't like that. He might look like a hippo, but he was always dangerous. More like a cobra—always ready to strike. Or maybe a combination of a cobra and one of the dirty river rats that Okot's little dog, Diling, used to hunt when they came into the village.

Okot had heard the cracking of Payne's whip every day since he was brought as a slave to Master Abbot's tobacco plantation. That was three months ago. Sometimes the whip was for him. Sometimes it was for Elisha, who slept in the cabin with Okot. Elisha was as old and black as an ebony tree, and his back was scarred and twisted from a lifetime of picking tobacco. Sometimes the whip was for Elisha's granddaughter, Mandy, who also slept in the tiny cabin with them. Payne liked to thrash Mandy when he caught her carrying water to the old men who were laboring in the fields.

Every day Payne's shouting, and the threat of his whip, roused Okot and the other slaves before sunrise. The work always went on until long after sunset, and Okot couldn't remember what it was like not to be tired. His back ached. His legs felt like lead weights. His eyes were gritty with dust from the fields. And he was always hungry.

Last night the slaves had been kept working later than ever. A big storm was coming, Payne told them. The master wanted as much work done as possible before the rain.

The moon was high by the time they were allowed to stop. Okot had stumbled back to his cabin and fallen onto his mattress in his shirt and breeches. They were scratchy with dirt and dried sweat but he was too tired to care. And now, Payne was whipping him for oversleeping.

Anger boiled up in Okot's stomach—so much fury that for a minute he forgot to be scared. He threw himself at Payne, kicking and flailing, shouting all the ugly words that he had learned from the overseer. Okot had no idea what he was saying, but he thought the words must be evil if Payne said them. Anyway, they felt good on his tongue. His forgot the pain from the whipping. He forgot about everything except how miserable Payne made his life. And he aimed a hard kick at the overseer's fat stomach.

Payne grunted like a pig wallowing in mud. He howled in pain and anger, dropping his whip and clutching his middle. Okot ducked around him and ran for his life. Across the bare yard and through the nearest gap in the poplar trees, down the hard-packed dirt track and into the tobacco field. The first streaks of sunrise were just lighting the sky. He ran like a gazelle with a lion after it, to where the other slaves were working. Every second he expected to feel Payne's arm on his shoulder. But the overseer didn't follow.

All day long Okot waited for Payne's shadow to fall on him. Every time he bent over to pull another weed the scabs on his back cracked open and bled again. Clouds of flies kept landing on his sores, buzzing like bees and smacking against his salt-streaked face like the sharp drops of rain in a storm on the African savannah.

All day long he wondered why Mandy and Elisha had left him sleeping. They must have known he would be punished. But he didn't see either of them in the field, so he couldn't ask.

And all day long Okot dreamed about the time before he was captured, when his days passed in the easy rhythm of herding his cattle on the wide grassy plains around Nyamlel. He thought of the cooking fires in the dark African nights, and the faces of the women shiny with sweat as they stirred their pots. Every day there were gourds full of fresh milk from their cows, plenty for everybody, and yams from the dark earth, cooked in the ashes until they were hot and tender inside their blackened skins. There was fruit—mangoes and bananas and dates— and cassava porridge sweetened with wild honey, and sometimes fish from the teeming river Lol….

Through the long evenings his brothers and sisters would giggle over their games, or curl up close to the smoky fire to keep away the mosquitoes and tsetse flies, listening to the songs of the women as they cooked and served supper to the men. The reflections of the flames would dance on their long bare legs, and on the sleeping huts up on their stilts, with the sweet-smelling grass sleeping mats and soft cowhide bedding waiting for them. And his father would be celebrating with the other men of the village or with visitors from across the river. There was always something to celebrate in those days—a marriage, or a good crop, a new baby, or twin heifers born to a favorite cow….

But Okot's father was dead. The slave raiders had shot him dead with his spear still in his hand. Africa was far away, across a salt sea so wide that Okot knew he could never cross it again. He had nothing left. No mother or father. No friends. He didn't even have his own name anymore.

The first day at the plantation, Master Abbot had told him that all his slaves had "decent Christian names." Whatever that meant. "Your name," Master Abbot said to Okot, "is Benjamin." And even though Okot told all the other slaves that his real name was Okot Deng, they never called him anything but Benjamin.

By the time the sun was high overhead Okot wanted to die. Every muscle screamed in pain. The biting flies were a constant misery. When he slapped and scratched at them it was worse, because the juice from the tobacco leaves stung his skin. He was so hungry that he tried to eat one of the leaves, but it was bitter and he spat it out.

Finally the golden sun sank low in the west. In the red twilight Okot started to see strange things. He thought ants had crawled up his legs, and it felt as though they were chewing a hole in his stomach. Once, he heard a calf bawl for its mother, and he thought he could see his family's little herd, and the soft steam rising from the plains of Nyamlel after a rain. But when he blinked hard, they were gone. There was nothing but the endless fields of this place called Virginia, and the thick rows of bitter tobacco plants.

Okot didn't remember coming in from the field that evening. One of the other slaves found him unconscious on the ground, and carried him back to the cabins. An old woman bathed his burning face and helped him to sip some cool water. When he was strong enough to sit up, she gave him cornbread soaked in milk. It was the best thing Okot had tasted since his capture, and he smiled his thanks. He knew she must have risked a whipping to get him the milk.

He wondered why he hadn't been punished. There was still no sign of Mandy or Elisha, but he didn't dare ask about them. When a slave disappeared, the others only rolled the whites of their eyes and looked away. Anyone who had an answer was asking for trouble with Payne.

The only slave Okot really talked to was Mandy. She was different from the others. Her skin was lighter than theirs. Her mother had died when she was a baby, and no one knew who her father was, so Elisha had always looked after her. She was thirteen, almost a woman, but her body was thin and hard, and her face had lines on it like an old man's.

Mandy was the only good thing in Okot's life. The first night after he arrived at the plantation, he woke up screaming from a nightmare. Mandy was kneeling beside him, washing his forehead with cool water. Many times since then she had rubbed warm pig grease into the sores that Payne's whip made on his back and legs.

Mandy's hands were gentle, and she always sang as she worked. Her voice was the sweetest sound Okot had ever heard. "Swing low, sweet chariot, comin' for to carry me home...."

Okot didn't know what a chariot was, but he understood the word "home." When he fell asleep again, he dreamed of the savannah around Nyamlel glowing in a golden mist through the long rains, and of his sisters tending their cassava patch under the hot African sun.

Now Okot was worried about Mandy. She'd never been gone so long before. What if Payne had done something to her? What if Master Abbot had sold her? How could he stand life on the plantation without her kindness and her songs?

Not even Okot's worries about Payne and Mandy could stop him from falling asleep that night. But sometime in the darkness Mandy crept back into the cabin. "Benjamin," she whispered, shaking his arm. "I have to talk to you."

Okot sat up, instantly awake. In the pale moonlight he saw that Mandy's face was swollen and bloody. Her sackcloth dress was torn at the shoulders. "What happened?"

"Shhh," she hissed. "Elisha's brother died. He was a garden slave. We was meetin' to have a Christian service for him. Payne didn't like it. He chained us up with the pigs."

"No!"

"Shhh! No matter. I like the pigs. Better'n Payne, anyway. But I had to tell you I'm sorry you got whipped 'cause of it."

"You want worse trouble? How'd you get out?"

"I can slide out of his shackles." She showed him her thin brown hands. "But I got to get back. Don't want him to know."

"Mandy, wait." Okot held her back. "I kicked Payne. Whyn't he whip me tonight?"

"Guess he was too busy with me and Elisha."

Okot shuddered. He said, suddenly, "Mandy, you ever think of runnin' away?"

"Hush, Ben!" Her eyes were wide. "Course not. This is my home."

"But Payne beats you. An' we never gets enough to eat. The master's dogs get better'n we do."

Mandy pushed his hand away. "Elisha's got no one but me now. If I run away, the master himself'd thrash him till he died. God put me here. That's all right with me."

"What's God?"

"Ben! Don't you never listen in church?"

"It don't make no sense to me."

Every Sunday, all the slaves had to sit on hard benches in a square cypress-wood building next to the family graveyard. Master Abbot or another man stood on a platform and gave the slaves their Sabbath instruction. They said things like, "Slaves, obey your masters. This is the word of the Lord." Every week, it was the same thing. "If you lead good lives, then you will escape from the punishment to come." But every week the punishment came all the same.

"This God," Okot said, "He be for white people."

"God is for all of us," Mandy said. "He made us. He takes care of us."

"Not me."

She sighed. "You too, Ben. How else d'you think you came here, when so many of the people died on your slave ship?"

"Maybe I'd better've died."

"Don't never say that, Benjamin. God's always got a reason for what He does."

"He got a reason for Payne whippin' me? Cause he's gonna whip me tomorrow for sure."

"Maybe he'll forget. Goodnight, Ben."

But Payne didn't forget. The next morning, he whipped Okot with a hickory switch. His face was red as an African sunset, and screwed up with fury so that his eyes were only little slits in his fat greasy cheeks. Afterwards he sent Okot back to work in the field.

As soon as Okot thought no one was watching he slipped away into the woods. He squatted against a tree in the leafy shadows, feeling sick and ashamed. If he'd had anything to eat, he would have thrown up, but his stomach was empty and it just cramped up. He wrapped his arms around his middle, shivering. There was only one thought in his head, pounding like the beat of a war drum. Payne had won. He had made him cry.

Okot was so still and quiet that the little forest creatures came out and scampered around his feet. They were like river rats, but with big, bushy tails. They carried nuts in their fat cheeks and cracked them open with their heads cocked to one side. Sitting under the tree watching them, Okot thought, *if they can live in the woods, so can I.* And he began to think about running away.

Chapter 2

Seeds in the Wind

"You're robbing me blind, Payne—killing off my slaves like this! I should take it out of your wages!"

Okot, Mandy, and Elisha could hear Master Abbot's furious shouting over the sound of rain drumming on their cabin. The big storm had finally arrived and all the slaves were shut indoors. The rain leaked in through cracks in the tin roof and whitewashed walls. It dripped onto their straw beds and turned the dirt floor to mud. But Okot was happy to have a day without work in the fields.

The master and his overseer were in the yard, wrapped in great wide capes that flapped in the wind. For once it was Payne who was being yelled at. The two men were standing by a rough wooden coffin. Master Abbot had let Elisha make it when another slave died. But this slave, a young man named William, had died because Payne hung him up by his thumbs and beat him to death.

Payne said William had been trying to escape. William, screaming in agony, swore he was only going into the woods to go to the toilet. When he died, Master Abbot was furious. "He was my best worker!" he roared. "You fool! I've a mind to whip you myself!"

Okot was watching through a knothole in the door. He gasped when the master jerked the whip out of Payne's belt. "Mandy, look!"

But Mandy, who was sewing a patch onto Elisha's shirt, shook her head. She was singing softly, the same familiar song: "I looked over Jordan and what did I see, Comin' for to carry me home? A band of angels comin' after me...." Elisha was reading from a battered old book that he called a Bible, and he didn't look up either.

Okot turned back to his spy hole. But Master Abbot only threw down the whip in disgust and marched off to the plantation house. When he was out of sight, Payne picked up the whip from the mud. He snapped it at the coffin as if he were hitting a slave. Then he spat on the ground and stomped away.

Okot sighed and hunched himself up on his damp bed. He was shaking with cold and wished he had a soft cowhide to wrap himself in like the one he used to sleep on in Nyamlel. To distract himself he looked over again at Elisha. What was it about this person called God, who Mandy said spoke to them in that book, and who was with them every day? How could He be with them, Okot often wondered, when he'd never seen Him?

Mandy had explained that she and Elisha, and some of the other slaves, were Christians. "That means Jesus is our Savior."

"Who's Jesus?"

"He's God."

Okot turned from Elisha and said to Mandy, "What's it mean, Jesus is your Savior?"

She put down her sewing. "It means Jesus took the punishment for everything I deserve to be punished for."

"You mean like whippin'? But you get punished plenty, even for doin' nothin'."

"But Jesus took the big punishment. He died for me."

Okot's eyes grew wide. "You mean you ain't never gonna die?"

"Yeah, sure. But then I get to a better place. Heaven."

Okot felt the scabby cuts and bruises on his back. "Don't take much to be better'n here."

"Better to be a slave here, and trust Jesus, than be a fine free gentleman like Master Abbot and goin' to hell."

For once, Mandy was not smiling when she said this. Her face was so serious that Okot didn't dare ask her what "hell" meant. Instead, he said, "Say, Mandy, what's these angels that you be singin' about? Can they take *me* home too?"

She smiled then. "Angels is God's messengers, Ben. Some people thinks that, when we die, we's gonna be carried to heaven on angels' wings."

She looked happy when she said this, but Okot sighed. "Home" couldn't mean Nyamlel, then. He couldn't get back there on angels' wings.

Ben. Benjamin. Slave. Okot. *I got as many names as this God of Mandy's,* Okot thought. *But what difference does it make what they call me? None of them care about who I am.*

He was jerked out of his thoughts by Payne's voice roaring at him. "Slave! You! Get up to the house. Missus has work for you."

It was a week after the storm. Laboring in the tobacco fields had been a sloppy and miserable job. Okot couldn't believe his luck—getting called to work at the plantation house.

Mrs. Abbot was reading in a swing chair on the veranda, but she looked up when Okot approached. "Hello, Benjamin." Her voice was nearly as warm and soft as Mandy's, and her great billowing skirts rustled like leaves in the dry season in Africa. A wide white hat shaded her face.

Okot waited at the bottom of the steps. He held his cap in his hands, the way he had been taught, and hung his head. He had learned that he could be whipped if a white person thought he wasn't showing enough reverence. He didn't know exactly what "reverence" meant, but he knew it had something to do with looking at the ground.

Mrs. Abbot came down to meet him. "They tell me you speak very good English."

Okot licked his dry lips. "A little, Ma'am. 'Tis a powerful strange tongue."

She laughed, and suddenly she seemed like a pretty young girl. She said, "I thought French was strange when I tried to learn it. Come. I want you to do some gardening for me."

Okot followed her around the plantation house. Beside it was a smaller building, made of the same red brick. The windows and doors were wide open. A great clattering and banging came from inside, along with the mouth-watering smells of roasting potatoes and meat. Okot's stomach growled.

"The vegetable garden needs tending," Mrs. Abbot said. "The slave—Elisha's brother—who used to do it, he died a couple of weeks ago. Do you know what to do?"

"Yes, Ma'am. I think so. We's had vegetable patches in Africa."

"Really?"

"We's like you, Ma'am. We's had cattle, an' grew our own food." Okot ducked his head again. He shouldn't have said that. She could have him whipped for speaking out of turn.

But Mrs. Abbot only shook her head. "Forgive me, Benjamin. I didn't know. All our other black people were born here in Virginia. Now." She waved at the garden. "You've got a lot of work ahead of you. Do your best. We have guests coming tomorrow night." She gave a silvery laugh. "I don't want them to think I can't run my own household."

Okot was looking at the book she had brought with her. It looked like the one that Master Abbot read from every Sunday on his platform. Was Mrs. Abbot one of these Christians too?

"Benjamin? Did you hear me?"

"Yes'm."

"Well, get on with it then." She sat down on a chair in the shade of a wide leafy tree, and settled into reading.

Okot trotted across the yard. A hoe stuck out of the soil halfway down a row of potato plants. He couldn't help thinking that Elisha's brother was the last person to touch it. The handle felt smooth and warm when he picked it up, as though the dead man had only put it down for a moment. Okot shuddered. Would the spirits be angry with him for touching a dead man's things?

"Benjamin!" Mrs. Abbot called.

Okot took a deep breath and wrestled the hoe out of the earth.

The garden was enormously overgrown, and the sun grew hot as he hoed the rich soil. It was a tricky job, pulling out the weeds without disturbing the tender lettuce plants or the root vegetables. Sometimes, when he stopped to wipe the sweat out of his eyes, he saw Mrs. Abbot looking at him. He wondered if he was working too slowly for her. But she didn't speak to him again.

Okot found the work comforting. He thought of the village women in Nyamlel, how their slender backs used to sway as they planted and weeded their vegetable plots. With a sigh Okot gathered up the heaps of weeds he had pulled out and dumped them, as Mrs. Abbot had told him to, over the fence at the edge of the garden. He could almost hear his mother's voice. She would have scolded any of the girls for piling the weeds so close by. "The seeds will come back in the wind," she would have said. "You have to take them away and burn them."

Suddenly he was angry with Mrs. Abbot. It wasn't fair that she should be able to sit peacefully here in her beautiful garden, when Okot's own mother had been sold as a slave, just like him. He often wondered where she was, and if she ever thought of him.

Just then a bell clanged. Okot looked up to see one of the kitchen slaves ringing the old brass bell by the back door. "Y'all c'mon now, boy," she called. "I's told to put out food for your dinner."

Mrs. Abbot looked up from her reading. "It's all right, Benjamin," she said. "You can eat now."

He came obediently, but under his breath he muttered fiercely, "My name is Okot Deng."

The kitchen slave had put out for him a cracked old plate with a slice of roast beef and a cold potato. But best of all, there was also a glass of milk. Okot drank it first, wishing there were more. Then he ate the potato and meat, crouched in a shady corner of the yard. When he finished, he turned his back to the kitchen windows and licked his plate.

Mrs. Abbot had gone into the house for her own dinner. Okot lingered for a while by the kitchen door, watching the slaves carrying full platters to the house, coming back with empty plates. His stomach still hurt with hunger. *They throw out more food than they give us to eat,* he thought resentfully. *Why can't they give me even a little more?*

The kitchen slaves all looked well fed. They wore white cloths on their heads and clean white aprons over their long dresses. Okot thought of Mandy's thin face and filthy sackcloth dress. Why was there such a difference between the slaves?

A huge dog lumbered out of the kitchen, and lay down beside Okot on the sunny steps. At first Okot was scared, but the dog moved stiffly, like an old woman, and after snuffling Okot it dropped its head between its paws and went to sleep.

"That be Gypsy," Elisha said that night, when Okot asked him about the dog. "She be big mastiff. Pet of Miz Abbot's. The master don't like that dog at all. Jest eats and sleeps. But Miz Abbot says Gypsy gonna stay."

The next day Gypsy was back again. She lay on the edge of the garden all morning, watching Okot work. After he ate his lunch, Okot let the dog lick his plate.

The sun was low in the sky when Okot finished hoeing the last row in the garden. His back ached, but not the way it did after a day in the tobacco fields. He leaned on the hoe and looked proudly at the neatly hilled rows of beets and potatoes, beans and peas.

Sometime in the afternoon, Mrs. Abbot had taken up her seat and book again. Now she called, "Benjamin, come here for a minute." Okot came, with Gypsy at his heels, and stood in front of her. She held up her book. "I want to read you something. Do you know what this is?"

"A Sunday book, Ma'am."

She smiled a little. "Why, I suppose so. It's a Bible. God's Word."

Mrs. Abbot opened the book and read out loud: "'There is no difference between the Jew and the Greek: for the same Lord over all is rich unto all that call upon him.'" Then she said, "Paul wrote that. What do you think it means, Benjamin?"

Okot had no idea what it meant. He didn't know anyone called Paul, and the words didn't make sense. He shook his head, being careful not to look Mrs. Abbot in the eye. "I don't know what's a Jew nor Greek, Ma'am. But I can see there's plenty of difference between black and white men."

"Never mind," Mrs. Abbot said. Okot thought she was speaking to herself. After a minute, she said, "I see you missed one of the weed piles. Throw it over the fence, and then you may go back to your cabin."

Okot did as he was told. But afterwards, he swallowed hard and stopped in front of her chair. "Ma'am?"

"Well?"

She was frowning, but Okot went on anyway. "Ma'am, you got to burn the weeds. See, the seeds come back on the wind. Grow again right away. You got to burn'em."

He thought, for a terrible minute, that she would call Payne. He shuddered. But instead, she nodded thoughtfully. "Of course. We'll do it tomorrow."

Gypsy tried to follow Okot when he went back to his cabin, but Mrs. Abbot called the dog back. Okot was sorry. He had started to like seeing the great dog whenever he looked up from his work.

Mrs. Abbot's words stuck in Okot's mind all evening. Why had she asked him what they meant? "There is no difference," the Bible said. Between men? *But there is,* Okot thought. *There's black and white. Slaves and masters.*

When he asked Mandy about it, in the darkness of the cabin after supper, she said, "It means we're all the same."

"But it ain't true. Even the slaves at the house is different from us."

"Men make us different, Benjamin. But we're not different to the Lord."

"Who's the Lord?"

"He's God."

God. Jesus. Savior. Lord. Okot frowned in the darkness. "He's surely got a lot'o names."

But Mandy didn't answer. She was asleep.

Okot couldn't sleep. The day's weeding had not tired him out the way that work in the fields did. He lay on his straw mattress, on his side because his back was still sore from Payne's whipping. The gentle noises of the night filled his ears. Chickens clucked in the yard, settling down to roost. Over by the sheds the pigs grunted and snuffled. Piglets squealed in the straw. There were voices, and the sound of horses clopping in the lane. The master's guests were leaving. The slaves who drove the carriages would be late getting to bed.

A whip cracked in the darkness and the horses broke into a swift trot. *At least the stable slaves get to hold the whips,* he thought. Another "difference" for his tired brain to think about. Okot stared at the tiny square of starry sky he could see through the cabin window. With all the talking and wondering about God and Christians and Mrs. Abbot reading from the Bible, he hadn't thought all day about escaping. It was time he started making his plans.

Where would he go? There was hushed talk sometimes among the slaves about the North. A land where they could be free. But how would he know when he was safe? Would the white men in the North send him back to Master Abbot, and to Payne's whip?

If I met a white man in the free North, Okot wondered sleepily, *could I trust him?* He pulled his ragged blanket up to his chin, shivering. Would he meet white people there who believed in Mandy's God? Would they see him just as a black slave? Or would they see him like the Bible said—no different? If he met a white boy his own age, could they be friends?

Chapter 3

Ambush!

Paul was alone, terrified, and very, very ashamed. How could he have left his father like that, surrounded by the Indians? They'd had war feathers on their heads. They carried lances and guns. They would kill him!

Paul collapsed over the sweaty neck of his horse, Storm. The big gelding snorted and shook his head. His flanks were heaving from their frantic gallop. The jingling of the bit made Paul's heart skip a beat. Had any of the Indians followed as he and Storm crashed through the thick forest? He strained his ears, but all around there was silence.

Which way should he go? On, until he found a white settlement where he would be safe? Or back? Paul's father, the Reverend Daniel Brentwood, was a Methodist circuit preacher. He was well known in this area of Upper Canada as a man of God. But sometimes that made it more dangerous for Paul and his father to travel by themselves. Some of the Iroquois hated the white man's religion that Brentwood preached. They were suspicious of Paul's white-blond hair and fair skin. They were even suspicious of the way the Brentwoods smiled so much of the time.

Paul was a long way from smiling now. But he knew what his father would do in his situation. He slipped out of the saddle and knelt on the ground. He asked God to keep his father safe. Then he mumbled another prayer. "Dear Jesus, I'm sorry I was a coward. Please help me." His face was still hot with shame, but he felt a little better.

Two hours earlier, Paul had been riding with his father along a rough wagon trail southwest of Brant's Ford. They traveled everywhere together, because Paul's mother was dead, and he and his father only had each other. Sometimes they stayed in white settlements, for a day or more at a time. They visited Indian villages and isolated homesteaders, and they went to the rough trading posts where Indians and white trappers traded fox and wolf furs, and beaver pelts. Today they had been heading for an isolated area that was just beginning to be cleared by English homesteaders.

Paul and his father had shared this life for more than two years, since they sailed from England to the New World when Paul was ten years old. That was just after the end of the War of 1812. Paul hardly remembered England now. This was the only life he knew, in this wild and exciting country.

Paul couldn't remember his mother. She had died when he was a baby. All his life he had grown up listening to his father talk about a place called Upper Canada, where there were savage people called Indians, and hardly any churches. Paul had always known that when he was old enough they would sail over the ocean to the New World. His father had told him about Joseph Brant, the famous Mohawk chief who became a Christian. His Indian name was Thayendanegea, which Paul still found hard to say. It always amazed him how easily the Mohawk language came to his father.

"God gave me a special love for the Mohawk people," Brentwood said, when he told his congregation in England that he was preparing to leave for the New World. "I knew it when Thayendanegea visited here. I was only my son's age then, but I knew I wanted to spend my life telling his people about our Savior." Paul still remembered how proud he felt when his father said to the congregation, "I asked the Lord to give me a strong son I could take with me to Upper Canada. And He did."

Paul loved the freedom of their life on the trail. Many of the homesteaders felt sorry for him because he didn't have a mother, but he knew he and his father were just fine alone. Every day they rode into new adventures. But today he and Brentwood were talking about a terrible thing. Iroquois had attacked a white settlement. They had killed and scalped everyone they found—women and children too, down to the tiniest baby.

One of the victims was Paul's best friend. Ever since Paul arrived in Upper Canada, he and Freeman had gone riding and camping together, learned to shoot and hunt together. They had built rope swings over the river on the edge of town, swum and swung and fished there, roasted their catch of trout on the riverbank and slept under the stars. And now, for no reason at all, Freeman was dead.

Paul kept kicking Storm to move on ahead of his father's horse. His face was twisted in a black scowl. Patiently, Brentwood kept catching up to him. Finally Paul burst out, "They're all murderers!"

"I know you're burning with hate, Paul. I hate what happened as much as you do. They were my friends too." Brentwood could never tell Paul now about one of the friends he'd lost in the massacre—the woman who had just agreed to marry him.

Paul saw the deep lines of sadness carved down the sides of his father's face, but he thought it was because Brentwood was unhappy with his attitude. "I guess you're going to tell me they're just sinners like us," he muttered.

"The Indians often have good reasons to resent what we've done to them."

Furiously Paul smacked a deerfly on Storm's neck. "*We* haven't done anything."

"I meant white men. But that's why they need to hear about forgiveness. We need God more than ever now. Only He is big enough to forgive all of us."

At that moment, without a breath of warning, a band of Indians on horseback burst from the wooded hill beside them! Storm shied violently, rearing and bolting before Paul had a chance to gather his slack reins. Whooping and hollering, the braves swept down at a full gallop, waving their guns and lances high overhead. Paul clutched Storm's mane and hung on desperately. Looking back over his shoulder he saw his father surrounded by the shrieking warriors. The last glimpse he had was of Brentwood's arm above the surging mass of horses and painted men—his right hand raised high in the sign of peace, while he held his terrified horse tightly reined in with his left.

And then Brentwood disappeared in the middle of the formless mob.

Paul bent low over Storm's neck, kicking the gelding's sides and giving him his head. Storm streaked for the opposite woods at a mad gallop. *Will they come after us?* Paul wondered as he dug his heels into Storm's heaving flanks. *Will they follow? Will they kill my father? Will they scalp us?*

It was getting dark. Paul felt as though he had been riding for hours, trying to find his way back to his father. At first he was sure he was following the trail that Storm had made in their wild gallop. But every few yards he stopped, puzzled. Everywhere he turned he thought he saw a path. Broken twigs, flattened grass. But after a minute or two he was lost again.

At last they came to a complete stop. Paul got off Storm. The horse rubbed his head against his chest, knocking him back against a tree trunk. "Poor fellow," Paul said, stroking his muzzle. "You're tired too."

Looking around him at the gloom of the forest, Paul shuddered. He had never felt so alone. Then he took a deep breath. *I'm almost thirteen,* he thought. *Almost a man. I can think my way out of this.*

Paul and his father had been traveling southwest when they were ambushed. Paul was sure that Storm had taken off into the woods to the east. So he had to go west to get back to the wagon trail.

Paul couldn't see which way was west because the forest completely hid the sun. *But I can tell which way is north,* he thought. The tree Storm had pushed him into was damp with moss. He was sure his father had told him that moss only grew on the north side of trees. He looked at several other trees nearby. They did seem to have moss only on one side.

It wasn't much of a trail, but it was better than not following any signs at all. Leading Storm, Paul set off toward what he thought was the west. Every few yards he stopped to feel for the moss. Finally the trees began to thin out. Patches of sky showed through the tops of the branches. Paul climbed stiffly back into the saddle. Storm plodded tiredly on. Then at last Paul saw the end of the forest.

His heart beat faster. Would he see his father? Had the Indians hurt him? He swallowed hard. What if they had scalped him? Paul shuddered. He wouldn't think about that. He dismounted and let Storm's reins hang down to the ground. His horse had been trained not to move when he was "rein-tied" in this way.

Holding his breath, Paul crept to the edge of the trees and peered out into the open country.

There was no sign of a fight. No sign of his father, or of the Indians. There was no horrible scalp mounted on a spiked stick by the wagon trail.

There was no trail at all.

Paul was not on the hillside where he had galloped into the forest. He was in a small clearing, surrounded by woods. There were no pathways leading out of it.

He was completely lost.

Chapter 4

Lost in the Bush

The summer evening was soft and warm, but Paul shivered. He was glad of Storm's bulky chest to lean against.

He took a deep breath. It would be all right. He had his oilskin and bedroll on his saddle. He had his little tin cooking pot and enameled mug, his water bottle and some food in his saddlebags. A faint trickling sound told him there was water close by. A fresh spring, or maybe even a stream. He would make camp for the night and find his way out in the morning.

Paul's father, and his friend Freeman, had both taught him it was best to camp in the open, where there was less chance of meeting the black bears that roamed the woods at this time of year. A bear with cubs was always ready to attack—and could kill a man with one blow of its great claws. Giant John Grant, a trapper the Brentwoods often met at the trading posts, had deep purple scars all down his back and one arm that he called "souvenirs" from a she-bear he once caught robbing his traps.

Even now, thinking about Giant John made Paul both smile and shiver. It wasn't only the Iroquois who sometimes hated the white man's religion. Many of the white settlers and trappers did too. Giant John was one of them. He led a wild kind of life. In the winters he traveled from post to post with his furs, usually in the company of an Indian brave from Ohsweken. At the trading posts he often got drunk, and ended up fighting with other Indians who were crazy with whisky. During the hot idle summers he picked fights with the white settlers instead. And there was no one he liked to argue with more than Paul's father. Whenever they met, at a trading post or a barn raising, Giant John was always getting at Brentwood, sneering at his religion and cursing him for preaching instead of doing what he called "a real man's work."

Rumors around the settlements said that Giant John had once killed a man. Paul could believe it. Just one glimpse of the trapper's brawny arms and chest, his glowering black eyes under fierce black eyebrows, could convince anyone that he was a violent man. Brentwood was tough himself—circuit preachers had to be—and he could stop John from fighting by holding the trapper's fists in a grip like a blacksmith's tongs. But Paul was still in awe of Giant John.

Every night the Brentwoods prayed for Giant John's soul. Thinking about that now, alone in the forest glade, Paul said a quick prayer for the trapper so that he wouldn't forget.

Storm shook his head and stamped impatiently. Paul patted his neck. "Sorry, fella." He led the horse around the clearing until he found the water. It was a little spring running over rocks into a mossy pool. Storm lowered his head and drank. Birds twittered in the trees. Storm's bit jingled as he lifted his head and blew gently against Paul's chest. It was so peaceful that Paul began to feel less like he was in trouble. It was a lot like the great camping nights he used to share with Freeman.

Brentwood had taught Paul to look after his horse first, no matter how tired he was. The previous circuit rider had frozen to death in a blizzard, because his horse went lame and he set out on the trail before the animal was sound again. "You mark my words, son," Brentwood said to Paul when he presented him with Storm. "The First Discipline of our church tells us, 'Not only ride moderately, but see with your own eyes that your horse is rubbed and fed.'" Paul thought guiltily that he sure hadn't ridden moderately today. He rummaged in a saddlebag for Storm's hobbles and fastened them around the horse's forelegs. They would keep him from straying more than a few yards in the night. Then he took off Storm's saddle and bridle.

The horse dropped his head and started grazing, tearing up tufts of fresh green grass around the spring. His coat was rough with dried sweat, so Paul pulled some swatches of long dried grass from the edge of the woods and rubbed him down. Then he spread out his oilskin near the water and opened up his bedroll on top of it.

Already he could hear the night noises of the forest. *First, a fire,* he thought. That would keep the bears away. He gathered dried leaves, old pinecones and small twigs from the edge of the clearing. They would make good tinder to start his fire.

From one of the saddlebags Paul took out his flint and steel. His father always insisted he carry his own flint. Next to a horse, he said, the most important thing to have in the wilderness was a way to light a fire.

Crouching by his heap of tinder, Paul struck a spark to it with his flint and steel. The resin in the pinecones caught the spark and soon he had a little fire going. He ran back and forth to the edge of the clearing, picking up fallen branches and pinecones until he thought he had enough to keep his fire burning through the night.

The light was fading. All around the clearing the sky over the trees was flaming red and gold. Paul still had no idea which way was west because the trees were too high and thick for him to see the sun.

He knew that his father would say, "Sufficient unto the day is the evil thereof." When Paul was a little boy, and he asked his nanny what that meant, she told him, "It means don't go looking for more trouble than you already have." So Paul thought, *I'll worry about finding my way out in the morning.*

He was so hungry that his stomach ached. Once the fire was burning brightly, he sat cross-legged on his bedroll and took out the food packed for him by the people they'd stayed with last night. It was supposed to have been their lunch, but they had fished in the river instead, and cooked fresh trout over a fire beside the wagon trail.

There was a hunk of fresh bread, and half a roasted chicken. "Thanks, Ma'am," he said out loud, remembering the kind woman who had given him and his father a room to sleep in the night before, and prepared the food long before sunrise that morning. He tore off a drumstick and chewed it while he examined the rest of the package. There was some of the inevitable pemmican—dried ground moose meat mixed with fat and dried currants—a small sack of salt, a twist of tea leaves, and—great bonus—a little whisky bottle filled with maple syrup.

"Hey, Storm," he called out. "My dinner's almost as good as yours." For dessert, Paul poured some of the sweet maple syrup over a piece of bread. Then he boiled up water in his enamel mug and made tea. The warm drink was comforting, and he wrapped his hands around the mug while he watched the fire and listened to Storm cropping grass. He thought of all the times he had done this with his father or Freeman, and his sense of adventure died a little. It wasn't the same alone.

He heaped the fire high with wood and then crawled into his bedroll. "Dear God," he whispered. "I know I'm big and strong for my age. But I wish I could be with my father. Please, Father God, help me through this night."

He was asleep before he got to the "amen."

Some time in the night a loud rustling woke Paul. He looked up, but he could only see two lights shining in the blackness. The fire had burned low. Slowly, his eyes adjusted to the dark, and in the pale moonlight he saw that the lights were the eyes of a deer, reflecting the red glow of the fire.

For a long moment they stared at each other. Then Storm whinnied. The deer whirled and leaped off into the bush, its white tail flashing as it bounded over fallen trees.

Paul grinned. The deer hadn't been afraid. There *couldn't* be any bears or wolves close by. He heaped more wood on the fire and curled up again in his bedroll. But then a disturbing thought came to him. The deer hadn't been afraid of him either, or of the fire. They must be a long way from any white settlement. For a second he felt even more alone than before. But then, in spite of his fears, he yawned. His father would say that God had a reason for what had happened. "I guess God can do the worrying for me," he murmured. He turned over in his bedroll, put his head on his arm, and slept.

Chapter 5

Run for Freedom

Okot woke up soaked with sweat and breathing hard. He was half excited, half terrified. Today was the day!

For nine months Okot had planned his escape. Whenever he had the chance while working in the tobacco fields he had slipped away into the woods. Each time, he looked at the nuts growing on the trees, and the berries. He noticed the ones the birds and squirrels ate, and the ones they never touched. He tasted the edible ones, and brought some back to the slave quarters, to ask what they were called. He learned about walnuts, beechnuts, and hazelnuts, red and black currants, raspberries and blackberries, gooseberries and black Concord grapes— everything he could find to eat in this new world.

Over the weeks and months Okot hid things in a hollow he found in a broad spreading oak tree. A leather pouch, with a few coins in it, that one of the Abbots' guests dropped one night in the laneway. A sharp little knife, which he stole from the plantation house kitchen. A small corked flask, with a leather thong, that he found among the hay bales in the stables—it was perfect for a water bottle once he poured out the amber liquid in it that smelled like strong medicine. He even had a flint and steel, for lighting fires, that he had found on the plantation house veranda after a garden party.

Okot knew he couldn't carry much with him when he ran away. But with a knife and a way to make fire he knew he could survive. He was *Monyjang*—a Dinka tribesman—and he would be free again.

Okot also learned as much as he could by listening to the older slaves. He found out where there were roads, and where there were only paths through the woods. He learned where nearby plantations were, and about the people who owned them. And all the time he learned to speak and understand more English.

Mrs. Abbot had decided that she wanted Okot to be her personal groom, to look after her horses and help her when she wanted to ride. So, through the fall, whenever he wasn't working in the vegetable garden, Okot spent his time at the stables. He was taught to feed and groom the horses. He learned how to saddle and bridle them, and how to help Mrs. Abbot mount and dismount. On rainy days he cleaned the leather tack, and polished the headlamps and the glossy black sides of the carriages.

Being around the stables gave Okot opportunities to hear news of the outside world. Every day the Abbots had visitors, white men who came with their slaves. Okot learned to listen in on conversations when they thought he was busy at his work. He heard the plantation owners talk about their troubles with slaves. Many slaves had escaped, and Okot found out that they were running to freedom in the North. If he could reach a place called Upper Canada then he too would be free.

Okot didn't say anything again to Mandy about wanting to escape. But she must have whispered his plan to Elisha. The old man never asked Okot about it. But there were times, when they worked together, that Elisha said things that could only mean he knew.

One cool night, when they worked late slashing down the tobacco leaves, Elisha suddenly put his arm around Okot's shoulder and looked up at the stars appearing in the night sky. His huge gnarled finger pointed to a brilliant diamond shining high overhead. "The North Star," he whispered. "The North Star to freedom. Many's a man who found his way home by followin' the North Star."

Okot had heard such things whispered by the slaves in the stables, but he had never understood what they meant. Now he knew. Elisha was telling him how to find his way when he ran away.

The old dog Gypsy was around Okot nearly all the time now. Some evenings when the Abbots had guests and the doors of the house were left open until late at night, Gypsy found her way to Okot's cabin and they curled up together on Okot's straw mattress. Mandy said once, "Master won't like that." But she often dragged her mattress closer to the two of them and slept with her back against Gypsy.

Life was better for Okot and all the slaves through the winter months. Once the tobacco harvest was finished then the work of hanging and drying the leaves was much easier than work in the fields. Many of the slaves were put to chopping wood and fixing fences. Okot had to muck out the horses' stalls in the stables every morning and night. It was easy work for him, and the warm smell of the horses reminded him of the cattle byres in Nyamlel.

Most days, Okot still worked for Mrs. Abbot up at the plantation house. Late in the fall he cleared the huge summer vegetable bed of plants and dug manure into the soil, ready for spring. Then he planted the winter vegetable bed, setting plants with strange names like Brussels sprouts and kale, parsnips and leeks.

The work wasn't so pleasant now that the weather had turned cold. Okot was amazed that he could see his breath steaming in the morning air, but his lungs hurt when he breathed. The green lawns wore a white coat of frost and the grass crunched under his feet. When he came around the corner of the big kitchen building a sharp wind stung his eyes, and working with the half-frozen soil made his thin fingers ache. He had been given a woolen shirt and cap to wear for the winter, but he was always cold. He wished he could feel the African sun again, hot on his back. He was really grateful now for Gypsy's company, and every day he ate his lunch leaning against the huge dog's warm side.

Spring came again, and Okot realized that he had been a slave for more than a year. He was twelve years old now, taller than ever, thin and tough as a hickory switch. At times, when the sun was warm on his back and his stomach full of good food, Okot thought that his life was not so bad after all. Maybe he was wrong to be thinking about running away. There were so many unknown dangers outside the plantation. He would be hungry again. And if Payne caught him he'd hang him up by the thumbs and whip him—maybe to death.

When he got to that point in his thinking, Okot knew that he had to be free—or die. He could never go back to Nyamlel, but he might get to that place in the free North where he could have his own vegetable patch, and his own little herd of cattle.

Every night Okot watched for the North Star to appear. At first he couldn't always find it. But once, when Mandy was grinding up some salt herring for them to have with their cornmeal mush for supper, Elisha took Okot away from the lights of the slaves' yard. He said, "You see those stars, boy? They makes a pattern in the sky. This one, it be called Ursa Major. The Great Bear. In him be the Dipper. See that, boy? See the handle, an' the cup? Them two bright stars, they's pointin' to our friend the North Star. Follow the line, boy? You see him burnin' so bright up there? Any man who follows him, God bring him home to the North, where he can be free."

Okot learned to see the stars that made the Dipper. After that he could always find the North Star. *Soon,* he thought, *I'll be ready.*

Overnight it seemed that the fair spring days turned hot and sticky. The heat reminded Okot of his home in Nyamlel—and so did the mosquitoes. But he knew how quickly the summer days would pass. The time had come for his escape. The next time Mandy and Okot were working close together in the tobacco field he told her he was going. She didn't tell him he was right or wrong. She just said, "I'll pray for you, Ben."

"Come with me."

She shook her head. "I told you, I can't."

"You gonna die here, Mandy."

"We all gonna die, Ben. I hope, wherever you get to, you find Jesus. Otherwise, you won't never be happy, even if you do get away from here."

"This Jesus, is He lookin' for me?"

"He's lookin' for all His lost children."

"I never saw Him yet."

She smiled. It made even her thin face beautiful. "You got to see Him with your heart, Ben. Not your eyes. Now get to work, before we both get whipped. Here comes Mister Payne."

The next day, Okot worked for Mrs. Abbot in the garden. They often talked together as he dug and hoed. Sometimes she read to him from her Bible, and showed him the words on the page. At first, the little black squiggles had been nothing but a blur to Okot. Now he could recognize some of the words.

This day Mrs. Abbot seemed especially unhappy about something. When she called Okot for his noon meal she said, "Listen to this, Benjamin." She read to him from her Bible: "'There is neither slave nor free man, there is neither male nor female; for you are all one in Christ Jesus.'" She put down the book. "What do you think of that?"

Okot squirmed. Mrs. Abbot always treated him with kindness, but if he said the wrong thing she could have him whipped. Finally he said, "Ma'am, there *is* slaves an' free men. I guess your Bible's wrong."

Bright tears like drops of starlight stood in her eyes. She said quietly, "I think we're the ones who are wrong."

The kitchen slaves didn't pay any attention to Okot now. He had learned to take his plate inside when he finished his lunch, so that he had a chance to look around for anything that might be useful. In this way he had picked up a discarded kerchief, and he used it to wrap the slices of meat he snatched when he could from the platters that came back from the master's dining room. "Y'ought not to, Ben," Mandy always said when he gave her the meat. "It's stealin', an' if you get caught, you'll get chained and whipped."

"It ain't stealin'. We work for our food," Okot insisted. "They owes it to us."

On the day before he planned to escape, he managed to steal several thick slices of roast venison from the kitchen. With that and his store of nuts in the leather pouch in the woods, he wouldn't have to find food for a day or two. He worked hard and fast all afternoon, so that he could get the gardening finished up. He had to be sure that he would be sent to the fields in the morning.

Okot felt a great lump in his throat when he patted Gypsy and waved goodbye to Mrs. Abbot in the evening. If his plan worked, he would never see either of them again. But Gypsy came to the cabin that night, and Okot slept snuggled up against the big dog, dreaming about stars and rivers and white men. In the morning Gypsy was gone. Okot's heart thumped like a drum against his ribs. But his mind was made up. He was ready.

In the middle of the morning he walked off boldly into the woods as if he were going to the toilet. No one looked his way. In a minute or so he reached his secret place. He had just finished tying the leather pouch to the string around his waist when a twig cracked behind him. He whirled around, his heart battering against his chest. But it was only Mandy.

"Ben," she whispered. "You gonna run now?"

"I got to, Mandy."

"You crazy. Payne'll kill you. He'll hunt you down with the dogs and kill you."

"You said we all gonna die, Mandy. I gotta die free."

"Wait till tonight. Please, Ben. It's safer."

He shook his head. "If I go in the night, Payne gonna whip you an' Elisha for sure. He'll say you heard me. This way, no one knows. Maybe it'll be all right for you."

They both knew it wasn't true. Payne would blame Mandy and Elisha anyway. Okot couldn't do anything else to help them.

Mandy sighed. "I thought you might do this. See, I got you a blanket." She rustled some dead leaves aside and took out a small gray roll, tied in strong twine. "The nights get cold real soon in the North. Not like here. Not like Africa." She pushed it into his hands. "Go with God, Okot Deng."

She was gone before he realized that she had given him a better present than the blanket. She had called him by his real name.

Okot knew that Mandy was right. As soon as he was missed, the Abbots' hounds would be sent to track him.

The Abbot plantation was on the south side of a wide river called the James. Okot had often studied the broad smooth stretch of water where it flowed by at the bottom of the long sloping lawns of the plantation house. He knew he had to get across the river as fast as he could so that the dogs would lose his scent.

"This be tidewater country," Elisha had told Okot. "It look easy, but there's strong currents. Many's a child drowned there in the springtime. No one wants to try'n cross the James after a lot of rain. Nor in the early year, when snow water comes down from the mountains. Even a strong man get carried out to the ocean."

Okot wasn't afraid of the river. He knew there were no crocodiles in it, as there were in the Lol River in Africa. As soon as he crossed safely, he would find a place to hide until night. Then he would start out following the North Star.

He ran swiftly through the woods to the river, making no sound at all. Not even the birds stopped singing as he went by. The little kitchen knife felt comforting, lashed to his side by a leather thong. He had venison in his pocket.

For the first time since the slave raiders came to Nyamlel he felt happy.

The sun was high in the sky when Okot reached the edge of the woods. Ahead of him was the James River. Thickets of twisted bushes grew along the bank. *The edges must be shallow,* Okot thought, *because rushes grew in the water, just like papyrus in the Lol River.* But to get to the bushes he had to run across a wide grassy space.

He looked up and down the river. In the distance on both sides he could see smoke curling from the kitchen chimneys of plantation houses. Across the river there were more woods. But could he get there?

There was no one in sight. All the fine families would be sitting down to their noon meal. Okot took a deep breath, ready to run low and fast the way his father had taught him in the savannah around Nyamlel.

Just then he heard the baying of dogs from the woods behind him.

Crouching at the edge of the woods, scarcely daring to breathe, Okot thought, *Mandy was right.* He should have waited until night.

Okot had once seen a fox that the hounds had cornered. If the dogs got him he would be torn to pieces just like a fox. He had to make a run for it now.

Just then there was a happy whining at his side. "Oh, Gypsy," he cried, as the old mastiff wriggled up to him. "What're you doin' here, girl?" he whispered, hugging the dog. "Oh, what'll I do now?"

His heart banged crazily in his chest. It was hard to think, hard to breathe. He would never get away now unless…unless he set the hounds a false trail. Shivering, Okot pulled off his shirt. It was nearly in rags, but somehow he felt even more defenseless without it. He wound the shirt into a thick rope and tied it around Gypsy's neck. He gave his faithful old friend another hug. "Go, girl," he whispered. "Go on, now. Go back home."

Gypsy whined and rubbed against Okot's legs. The baying of the hounds was louder. Okot could hear Payne shouting. "Go, Gypsy!" he said sharply, and pushed the dog away. "You gotta go, else we both be killed." He started across the open grass, and Gypsy followed him. "No!" he cried. He picked up a small stone and threw it at the dog. "Go home, Gypsy!" The dog yelped and whined. Okot threw another stone, and this time Gypsy turned and lumbered back into the woods towards the plantation.

"I'm sorry," Okot sobbed. "I'm sorry, girl." But there was no time to think about what he had done. He turned and ran for his life to the river.

The shallow edge of the water was choked with reeds and stiff stalks with furry brown tops. Okot waded through them, feeling the sharp leaves cutting into his skin. The river was dark and cold. It looked wider than it had from the plantation house.

Suddenly the hounds burst from the woods—two of them, straining against the leads that Payne held. Crouching low in the reeds, Okot saw the dogs hesitate and start sniffing the ground in circles. One wanted to follow Okot's path to the river. The other was sniffing at the way Gypsy had disappeared into the trees. Okot almost laughed out loud when he saw the dogs pulling Payne in different directions. But which one would the overseer believe?

Feeling underwater for his knife, Okot cut one of the hollow reeds and put it in his mouth. He sank down until the water covered his head. Breathing through the reed, he wormed his way upstream through the choking grasses. If the dogs followed him, he needed to get as far away as possible from where he had gone into the river. That way Payne might think he was already on the other side.

Okot knew he was safer staying underwater, but after a few minutes he had to know what was happening. Carefully he raised his head.

Master Abbot had joined Payne. The dogs were still running in circles, sniffing the ground. Finally, Payne let them go, and they bounded off toward the woods, following Gypsy's trail.

"He ain't here," Payne shouted in disgust. "He must've seen he couldn't cross the James. He's gone back to the plantation. Changed his mind."

"I never knew a runaway to change his mind," Abbot said. "He may be hiding in the woods, waiting for night. Keep looking."

They both turned back toward the woods, following the dogs.

Okot waited until they were well away before he swam across the river. It was a long and tiring swim. Three times the current sucked him under and he had to fight his way back to the surface, gasping and spitting out the muddy-tasting water. By the time he dragged himself up the far bank he had drifted a long way downstream. He was coughing and shivering, and his mouth was full of the taste of mud. But he had made it! He was on the north side of the James River. He was on his way to freedom.

Chapter 6

The Hunting Party

Chipagawana dreamed of becoming a great hunter and warrior brave of his people, the Haudenosaunee. His father, Thunder Arm, was wise and strong, one of the greatest war chiefs of their Onondaga tribe. His grandfather, Fleet Arrow was a distant cousin of the famous Chief Pontiac of the Matchenawtowaig tribe. Fleet Arrow was an old man now but his memory was still sharp. His eyes glistened as he told stories in the longhouse meeting-place of hunting trips from long ago. He talked about the wars he had fought with other tribes, and how he had led his people to victory.

He also told of the coming of the first white men. They wanted furs, fox and wolf and beaver, that the Indians could trap for them. They traded for the furs—beautiful beads that now decorated the buckskin clothing of the Haudenosaunee. But other white men came to take the land away. Many people died because the French and the English were fighting over the land. It was only two years since the last great war of the white men ended, and the Redcoats no longer trampled all over Haudenosaunee territory with their horses and their cannons.

Chipagawana was only twelve, but already he had learned much about the ways of the forest from his father, Thunder Arm, and from his older brothers, Swift Deer and Black Hawk. He knew how to track deer and bear. He knew what the howls of the wolves meant, and he could imitate them perfectly. He could imitate the songbirds too, a dozen or more of them from the cheeky chirping of the chickadee to the twee-twee-toyou-toyou-chack-chack-wheep-wheep of the thrasher. He knew what the silence of the songbirds meant, too—danger all around, or a storm brewing. He knew how to read the sky and the trees for signs of rain or snow. He had helped his brothers make a canoe from elm bark, and seal it with pine gum. All his life he had watched, and listened, and learned.

Thunder Arm and Fleet Arrow had taught Chipagawana to distrust white men, who only wanted to take more and more of the Haudenosaunee land. Warrior braves told Chipagawana terrible stories of the things white men had done. They had brought strange sicknesses that the Onondaga medicine men could not cure. "They had to be attacked," Thunder Arm said, "because they made the Great Spirit angry." They had to be stopped from taking the land that belonged to the Onondaga.

"They also brought whisky that takes away your mind," Chipagawana's grandfather said. "It makes a fool out of a brave. Don't touch it."

Sometimes, Thunder Arm went with other men from their clan, the Hotahyonhne, to the trading post. They took furs to trade for knives and cooking pots, beads and mirrors and woven cloth. Thunder Arm knew how to speak some French and English. He had never taken Chipagawana to the trading post, but he taught his son what he knew of the white man's languages. "The son of a chief," he said, "had to know how to speak to these people, for the good of the clan and the tribe."

Chipagawana secretly hoped he would never meet a white man.

Late in the summer when Chipagawana was twelve, Thunder Arm told his youngest son that he could go with the Hotahyonhne braves on his first long hunting trip. Chipagawana had longed to see the places the braves talked about, like the Thundering Waters between the great lakes that were called Niagara. That was two days' riding from their village of Ohsweken.

Chipagawana knew that his father was making him ready for the day that would come after his dream fast when he would ride with the other men of his tribe on the warpath. Then he would be a true Onondaga brave. His heart beat faster just thinking about it.

Most years, the long hunting parties did not go out until after the harvest. But Thunder Arm had studied the trees, and the birds and animals of the forest, and he said that the Great Spirit was going to send the winter early this year. There would be much snow and many deer would starve. "We must hunt early," he said, "and hunt well, so that we have enough meat for the long, hungry moons of wintertime."

Thunder Arm was a great marksman. He could shoot an arrow through a leaf at fifty paces. Chipagawana wanted his father to be proud of him on his first long hunt, so he began to prepare himself. First he spent days making extra arrows for his quiver. Each had a perfectly straight shaft of peeled wood. He carved one end, the way Thunder Arm had taught him, to hold the sharp arrowhead in place. He made a notch for the bowstring, and a slot for the feathers that would make the arrows fly far and straight. Then he rode out for long hours on his young paint horse, Proudfoot, to practice his shooting.

And he waited impatiently for the hunt to begin.

Finally the big day came. Early in the morning, while the grass was still wet with dew, the party gathered at the edge of the village palisade. There were fifteen men going on the hunt, all mounted on sturdy pintos. For eight days they rode in a great circle, going north first, then west, and finally south. They forded streams and went along old forest trails known to Thunder Arm and the older braves. Sometimes in the distance they saw smoke rising from some white man's settlement. They stayed well away, and avoided other Indian villages too.

They didn't have to go so far from Ohsweken to hunt, but Thunder Arm liked to explore new territory. Every night they camped in small valleys near clear rivers. The waters swarmed with trout that they caught and cooked over campfires. They shot rabbits and partridges too, and ate them roasted with cornbread baked on hot stones.

Once, in the stillness just before dawn, Chipagawana woke and saw a wild turkey at the edge of a small copse. Holding his breath, he fitted an arrow carefully onto the string of his bow and let it fly. It hit the bird near the tail. In the wink of an eye Chipagawana nocked and loosed another arrow. That one killed the bird. Thunder Arm and the other braves were astounded. Wild turkeys were so shy that they were almost impossible to shoot. "My son has special sight," Thunder Arm said. "It is a gift from the Great Spirit. Someday he will use it to save his people from great danger."

There was great feasting in their camp that day. Chipagawana was so proud he thought his heart would burst.

On the eighth night everyone felt a new sense of anticipation. Tomorrow they would begin the real hunt.

Fresh feathers were fitted into arrows. The air sang with the sound of knives being sharpened against wet river stones.

The older horses were veterans of many hunts and slept peacefully through the night, standing nose to tail and resting one hind leg after another. Proudfoot, though, was uneasy. Chipagawana rubbed his little paint's nose and ears, trying to calm him down. But his own heart was pounding so hard that he only made Proudfoot more restless.

The air was chill and gray with mist when Chipagawana woke the next morning. The braves moved like silent spirits through the camp, preparing themselves for the hunt. Chipagawana's hands shook with excitement as he strapped on his quiver of arrows and his knife.

The knife was a gift from his father. Thunder Arm had brought it back for Chipagawana on his last trip to the trading post. It was sturdy and sharp, with a strong bone handle, and Thunder Arm had carved into it Chipagawana's name, and the name of his Hotahyonhne clan. Chipagawana felt like a true brave with it strapped to his leg.

Finally, Thunder Arm gave the word and they rode into the gentle wind that had come up with the sunrise. Chipagawana rode with his father at the head of the party. As the braves spread further apart, they used birdcalls to signal each other.

Proudfoot trotted silently over the thick, springy grass. They were near the edge of a forest now. Wildflowers bloomed everywhere, and Chipagawana could see faint trails made by rabbits and foxes. The breeze was blowing stronger, gusting around them and making the branches of the trees sway and creak. The birdcalls from the hunting party were snatched away in the wind.

All at once, Chipagawana shivered. He had strayed too far and was being left behind. He slapped Proudfoot's neck with his reins and dug his heels into the young horse's sides. Proudfoot snorted and bucked and broke into a run.

Then Chipagawana heard a great whoop far away to his right. "Aiee!" the hunters yelled, taking up the cry. They were galloping from all directions toward Thunder Arm, racing in for the kill.

Proudfoot galloped as fast as he could back toward the hunters. Then suddenly he reared and shied with a terrified scream. They were face to face with a black bear!

Chipagawana fought to keep his frightened horse under control and draw his bow at the same time. Twang! He loosed an arrow blind and it hit the bear in the shoulder. Chipagawana knew he was in real trouble. The bear had been robbing honey from the hollow of a tree and the air was thick with bees. As Proudfoot bolted about in a mad frenzy, swarms of bees attacked Chipagawana, stinging him on the face and buzzing madly in his ears. The bear was enraged, twisting and biting at the arrow in its flesh. Chipagawana knew that at any moment it would charge, but he couldn't see to nock another arrow. He hauled Proudfoot's head around, lashing the horse's sweating flanks with the reins. The terror-stricken paint took off in a flat hard gallop.

Seconds later Chipagawana reined in Proudfoot. His face was sore from the bee stings and he could hardly see out of his puffy eyes. He didn't know what to do. He wanted nothing more than to run back to the hunting party. But Thunder Arm had taught him that a wounded animal was dangerous. It had to be killed.

Thunder Arm had just praised his son for his special gifts. Chipagawana didn't want to go back to his father in shame. A brave would do the right thing even if it put him in danger. Even if it killed him.

Chipagawana swallowed hard. He fitted an arrow in his bow and nudged Proudfoot into a trot. They were upwind of the bear now, so he took Proudfoot around in a huge circle until he could approach it from downwind. That way, he thought, he might get close enough to shoot it.

It was no good. In a flash the bear dropped to all fours and charged. Chipagawana shot his second arrow. It hit the bear in the head and bounced off. The creature didn't even notice. The third arrow missed altogether. Chipagawana swiped at the bees and strained to see through his swollen eyes. Proudfoot reared and lunged forward, past the bear, bolting for the shelter of the woods.

Just as Chipagawana thought they were safe he felt the great honey-crusted claws rake a burning path down his left thigh. Proudfoot screamed again—a hideous scream as the claws tore into his flank. He galloped for the forest with the bear right behind him and the bees still all around. Chipagawana clung to Proudfoot's back with his hands wrapped in the horse's mane, desperate to stay on though his left leg hung down uselessly. He couldn't see a thing now. Branches whipped his face and water streamed from his inflamed eyes. He crouched low over Proudfoot's neck and hung on for his life.

Chipagawana lay in a twisted heap on the forest floor. He didn't know how far Proudfoot had galloped before he lost consciousness and slid off. He didn't know if the wounded bear was still nearby.

He felt for his bow, and found he was lying on it. His knife was still strapped to his right leg. His left leg was hot and swollen from the hip to the knee and burning with pain. There was a long tear in his buckskin legging, and blood oozed from the gouges. Flies buzzed all around him.

Finally Chipagawana lifted his head. It felt heavy and throbbed as though he were inside a drum. He brushed away the flies and his hand came back covered in hot sticky blood. The skin had been slashed open across his forehead and down his right cheek, by a branch or maybe by one of the sharp slate rocks that poked up through the pine needles on the ground under him. He sat up stiffly. He tried to stand but cried "Aiee!" as pain shot through his leg. He sat with his back braced against a thick tree trunk.

There was not a sound in the woods. Not even a bird sang. Chipagawana felt the hairs stand up on his neck. *Danger!* he thought, and gripped the handle of his knife. Was it the bear? He strained his ears. Nothing moved, not even the branches in the trees.

Then he heard it. The faintest sound, like a whisper. Something was moving in the dried leaves of the forest floor. He strained to see into the shadows through his puffy eyes. The sunlight made spots like silver raindrops in the air.

Chipagawana froze at the sudden buzzing noise. He knew it wasn't more bees. It was a rattlesnake. Sweat poured down his face. Then he saw it, slithering on the edge of the shadows toward him. It was huge, as long as two arrows, and thick around as a man's arm. He could see the unmistakable orangey-brown pattern on its back. The long forked tongue lashed in and out of its flat head, close enough for Chipagawana to touch.

There was a movement just behind Chipagawana. Out of the corner of his eye he saw a rabbit. It stopped beside the tree trunk, petrified with terror at the sound of the rattle. Then the snake struck. It moved so fast that Chipagawana saw nothing but a blur. The rabbit squealed. Chipagawana saw it twist and fall over, jerking in the spasms of death, and he squeezed his eyes shut. When he opened them again, both the snake and the rabbit were gone. His hand let go of the knife.

The sun was beginning to set. Chipagawana shivered, and waited. He hoped that Proudfoot would come back. The hunting party, he knew, could be very far away by now. Thunder Arm wouldn't know where to look for him. Chipagawana licked his dry lips and tried a few of the birdcalls that he knew Thunder Arm would recognize. But there was no answer.

He had never been so thirsty, or in so much pain. But he was the son of a chief. *I know the forest,* he thought. *I can look after myself.*

With a great effort Chipagawana used a low branch to pull himself to his knees. Huge cedar trees surrounded him. He pushed dead needles and small twigs together to make a base, and then broke off enough fresh young branches to cover the twigs, making himself a soft dry bed.

He lay down and pulled more branches over him. That was better. But his wounded leg burned with a raging fire.

Stars twinkled faintly through the high tops of the trees. *This land belongs to the Great Spirit,* Chipagawana thought. *Can the Great Spirit help me now?* He felt very small in the dark forest. He wished that he had already gone on his dream fast. Then the Great Spirit would already have come to him and showed him the animal that would be his special guardian for the rest of his life. *If I knew my guardian animal,* Chipagawana thought, *I wouldn't be all alone now.* But the time for his dream fast was still two years away.

He took a deep breath, filling his lungs with the fresh resiny smell of the crushed cedar. The burning in his leg began to spread until he was hot all over. The stars looked so close, and cool as ice on the lakes in wintertime. Burning pain and thirst became his whole world. *Will Thunder Arm find me?* he wondered. *Or will I die here, in the forest, all alone?*

Chapter 7

North by Starlight

Five days after his escape Okot woke up to a wild storm. He had found a shallow cave that morning to sleep in, but the wind lashed the entrance, driving torrents of rain right to the back wall. He had just decided that he might as well travel on, since he was getting wet anyway, when a black shadow moved across the entrance. A bear cub.

It looked a lot like a big cuddly dog, but Okot had learned from the other slaves at the plantation how dangerous bears were. He flattened himself against the cave wall, holding his breath. The cub seemed to sniff around for ages, and finally it waddled in. It smelled like a wet blanket and snuffled just like old Gypsy did around the plantation house kitchen. Okot bit his lip and tried not to tremble. Outside, the storm thrashed the trees and lightning split the heavens. Okot imagined he could see the spirits of ancient tribes fighting in the air around him.

Just when he thought he couldn't stand still for another second, there was a growl outside the cave. His heart banged wildly. *Dear Jesus God,* he thought, *if you're really here to take care of me like Mandy said, please don't let me get eaten by a bear when I've only just escaped.*

With a little bound the cub padded around and disappeared out into the woods with its mother. It took

Okot a few moments to believe that they were really gone, and to start breathing again.

After that experience Okot stayed out of caves. He slept instead during the days in any thick clump of bushes he came across at sunup. During the nights, while he ran on his long, tireless legs, he often thought about his prayer to Mandy's Jesus God. He wondered why he had suddenly prayed like that. But mainly he wondered if this strange God had really heard him and sent the bears away.

On the fourteenth day he was woken by the sound of voices. He had curled up that morning in a dense grove of dogwoods near the edge of a pond. Now he peered out carefully. The sun was high overhead and five or six boys were taking turns on a rope swing, shouting and laughing as they skimmed across the water and splashed down into the middle of the pond.

Okot blinked hard. For a moment he thought of his friends in Nyamlel. Were any of them still alive? Did they still swing from the tamarind trees like monkeys, and go fishing together? *Will I ever have friends again?* he wondered.

The boys had stripped off their clothes to swim, and their skin flashed white in the sunlight. The clothes were scattered all over the grassy bank. Okot could almost reach the nearest shirt. Holding his breath, he wriggled forward, closer to the edge of the bushes.

"Quick! C'mon! I see him!"

The shriek came from so close by that Okot's teeth chattered with fear. It was all over. He could never escape now. Should he crawl out into the open? Or wait for them to come in and get him?

He had just decided to give himself up when a young girl ran by his hiding place. Another followed, holding up her skirts and giggling. "Hey, Jeremy!" the first girl shouted. "Y'all want to show us your fine new clothes?" But the boys were already scrambling up the far bank of the pond as fast as they could go. One turned and yelled, "Get away, Caitlin! Mama'll lick your hide if we tell her you was out here."

"What about you, skippin' your chores?"

"I ain't!" he shouted before disappearing into the trees with the other boys.

The girls, laughing, picked up as many of the clothes as they could carry. "Should we throw'em in the pond?" the second girl asked.

The one called Caitlin shook her head. "Let's just hide'em," she whispered. To Okot's astonishment she shoved the whole bundle into the dogwoods, almost on top of him! The other girl did the same, and then they ran around the pond and into the woods after the boys.

Okot was so surprised that he wasted several seconds just lying under the avalanche of clothing. He had to put his fist in his mouth to stop himself from laughing out loud. He thought of Mandy saying that her God would take care of him. *If this is how God works,* Okot thought, *then He's a mighty useful God.* As fast as he could, he pulled on a pair of homespun breeches and a checked flannel shirt. They were too short, and they billowed out on his thin body. But they were warm and soft and nearly new. None of the shoes would fit on his long, narrow feet, but that didn't matter. His worn old leather slippers were fine.

What mattered now was getting away as fast as possible. Okot rolled his blanket up tightly, pulled his cap low over his forehead, and crept out of the thicket. Silence. He crouched down and ran for the trees.

"Hey!" someone shouted. "Look, it's a black man!"

"He's wearin' my clothes!"

"I bet he's a slave!"

"Runaway!" they all shrieked.

Once again Okot ran for his life. The boys came after him, running from the other side of the pond. "Jeremy, wait!" one of the girls cried, and Okot ran faster. He could hear them crashing through the trees behind him. But none of them was a match for Okot. In no time they fell far behind. Soon the only sound in the woods was Okot's ragged breathing.

He didn't dare stop. The word would be out. It wouldn't be long before all the farmers and plantation owners in the area were out looking for a runaway slave. Would they chase him with dogs? Could he escape again?

Okot thought he should stop running and hide. He didn't even know which way he was going. But he was too scared to stop. He wanted to put as many miles as he could behind him.

After a while, the sun had moved far enough into the afternoon sky for Okot to tell he was running mostly to the west. He turned as much north as he could in the dense trees, and soon he came to the edge of the woods. He shrank back behind a thick oak tree and peered out at the open land.

He was at the side of a long roadway. It looked like one of the lanes on the Abbot plantation. There was a stable and yard off to the right, with horses grazing in the field. Further along, standing on its own, was a tall wooden building with no windows. He could smell the hickory smoke that drifted on the breeze from a huge chimney in the center.

"The smokehouse," Okot whispered to himself. His stomach rumbled painfully and for a moment he forgot about the danger he was in. He thought about the hams and beef quarters that would be hanging inside, along with bacon and smoked turkey, game birds and venison.

Since his escape, Okot had sometimes been ashamed of how much he craved meat. In Nyamlel he had hardly eaten anything but milk and cheese, fruit and cassava, and he'd thought nothing could be better. But now, just thinking about beef or ham made him drool.

Suddenly he pulled back into the trees. Two men were walking along the roadway from the stables. They wore capes and carried walking sticks. As they came closer Okot could hear them talking. "You're a fool, John. I say so even if my Bible says I shouldn't. Free labor is nothing but trouble. We need the slaves."

"Slavery is wrong, and God will judge us for it, Martin," said the other man. "I for one intend to put things right. I won't own slaves again."

"Then you should learn to lock up your house and barns," Martin said. "Starting with your smokehouse."

"If a man is in that much need of a slice of meat that he'd rob me, then I'd just as soon let him have it."

"Then he will," said Martin. "Really, John, you belong in Upper Canada with the other Loyalists."

"We got as far as Erie once," John said. "But the missus took one look at the ship and said there was no way she was going to cross the lake in that rat-infested schooner."

The men laughed and walked on. *They still have slaves here,* Okot thought, watching them. *But at least I must be going in the right direction.* But what was "Erie"? Did he have to cross another lake to get to Upper Canada? Would it be like the wide salt ocean he had come across from Africa? "No," he whispered fiercely. It couldn't be. Upper Canada was not that far away. Elisha would have known. But then, what did the man named John mean?

At last, Okot shrugged. He would find out sooner or later. When the men were out of sight he darted across the lane. The wooden latch on the smokehouse door lifted easily, and he slipped inside. It was cool and dark and it took a minute for Okot's eyes to adjust to the gloom. He saw huge hams hanging by ropes from the rafters, and beef haunches, just as he remembered from the Abbots' smokehouse. A low, smoky fire burned in the fire pit in the middle of the floor.

Okot took out his knife and put the handle between his teeth. He climbed up a few rungs of the sturdy wooden ladder that was leaning against one wall. Stretching as far as he could, he cut a great hunk off one of the hams. It fell to the floor with a dull thud. Quick as a cat after a mouse, he jumped down and picked it up. He hacked off a slice and ate it right there, crouching by the fire. It tasted of hickory and apple wood, rich and honey-sweet, and he thought he could never have enough of it. When he was finally full to bursting he licked his fingers and stuffed the rest of the ham into his leather pouch. Then he had a drink of water from his flask and wondered what to do next.

All at once he was overcome by an enormous yawn. He had run all night and half the morning with only a couple of hours' sleep. The heap of empty grain sacks in one corner looked so inviting that he decided the best thing was for him to sleep there until nightfall. He made a bed with a few of the sacks and then pulled the rest over him, so that he would be hidden if anyone came in. He was asleep as soon as he closed his eyes.

It was a cloudy night when Okot slipped out of the smokehouse door. No moon shone in the sky and there were no stars to show him his way. The wind howled around the corner of the building and moaned in the trees across the roadway. Okot shuddered. Which way should he go?

First he had to get back into the woods, where he could hide and think about what to do. He took a deep breath and turned the corner, ready to make a dash for the trees.

"Boy! Stop right there!"

The light of a lantern blinded Okot. Someone grabbed his arms from behind. "Well, Martin, you were right," the man with the lantern said. "What do you suggest I do with him?"

"A strong boy like him, John—there must be an owner not too far away who's sorely missing his property."

"You know I don't like that kind of talk, Martin, even if you are my friend."

For a moment the lantern swung away from Okot to the other man's face. Okot felt the grip on his arms loosen. In a flash he had wriggled out of the huge, billowing shirt and he ran across the laneway toward the woods. He stumbled once in the darkness but kept going. Every second he expected the men to follow. But when he reached the shelter of the trees he heard the man called John saying, "Let him go. Did you see those welts on his back? Someone's treated him foully, Martin. I wish the best of

God's fortune to him. I'll not be responsible for tracking him down."

Okot shivered as the cold wind bit into his bare back. But he grinned to himself. *At least,* he thought, *I'm still free. And that man won't set anyone's dogs after me.* He unrolled his blanket and wrapped it around his shoulders. Then, when his eyes had grown accustomed to the dark, he trudged off into the woods. He found a great spreading oak tree with thick leafy branches, and climbed it until he was certain he was hidden from the ground. There he settled down in a wide notch and waited for the wind to blow the clouds away.

The nights were getting longer and cooler. Okot didn't know how long he had been running, but his life on the plantation seemed far away, as though it had happened to someone else. He was wise now in the ways of white men, and he had learned to spy out the great houses early in the mornings. This way he had managed to steal another shirt after a black woman pegged out the household laundry. Once, growing bold because he was so hungry, he took a hot meat pie right off the ledge of a kitchen window. He was chased off by a scruffy little terrier dog, and he had to give it some of the pie so that it would stop barking.

Sometimes Okot came to main roads, but the signposts meant nothing to him. He swam across several wide rivers, one of them so swift and icy cold that he was certain he would drown. He climbed steep hills and slithered down deep green valleys. But he had not yet come to the lake that the men John and Martin had talked about, or the place called Erie.

One evening Okot crept up on a clearing by the side of a road where several wagons had stopped for the night. A dozen or so men were eating stew or drinking coffee out of battered tin cups around a brightly burning campfire. The good hot smells reminded Okot that he hadn't eaten anything that day but a few wormy green apples from an abandoned orchard. He hid himself in a dusty clump of bushes and listened.

The men's voices carried far in the clear night. They talked about the price of cotton and tobacco, and the possibility of steamships coming to the Great Lakes. But one man said something that made Okot's heart beat faster. "When I get this load of cotton loaded onto the schooner at Erie, I'm finished with this life. Gonna sell my team and settle down to farming."

Some of the men laughed, and one said, "Farming's a harder life than this." But Okot strained to see the man's face in the firelight. *Erie!* This man was going to Erie, and his load was going on a schooner. It must be going to Upper Canada!

The men sat, it seemed for hours, around the fire. Okot was cramped and stiff by the time they finally went back to their carts and wagons to sleep. But he was cheered by what he saw. The wagon headed for Erie was piled high with great bales wrapped in burlap. It would be easy to hide in the middle of those. He waited until the drivers had all settled down to sleep, and then he slipped around behind the wagon and climbed on board. It was dusty as he wriggled his way into the middle of the stacked bales, and he had to rub his nose hard to stop himself from sneezing. But in the middle he found a clear area, just big enough for him to lie down in if he curled himself into a ball. The bales made solid, comforting walls. He wrapped himself in his blanket and smiled up at the stars in his little patch of open sky.

They set off before dawn. The wagon lurched and rumbled along all that day, and the next. Once it rained and Okot huddled under his blanket, wet, cold and miserable. He took tiny sips from his water bottle and tried not to think about how hungry he was. At last, late on the second evening when he began to think the journey would never end, he heard the sounds of clattering hooves and shouting voices that must mean they were coming into a town.

Okot's patch of sky was black by the time they stopped. He wormed his way to the front of the wagon and peered cautiously out between the cotton bales. He could see water twinkling in the moonlight, and dark shapes that must be ships bobbing up and down in the evening breeze. But there was no time for more than a glimpse. Already the wagon was being jostled as the bales were unloaded. He had thought they would wait until morning. Now what was he going to do?

Straining as far forward as he could, Okot tried to see around the corners of the bales. There was no one in sight. With his heart in his throat he wriggled out headfirst and dropped to the ground, ducking under the wagon and crouching behind one of the wheels.

A couple of stocky men were carrying the bales down a gangplank and onto the ship the wagon driver had called a schooner. Another man on board was handing them down a wide opening in the deck. *I have to get in there,* Okot thought. *But how?*

It was the wagon driver himself who came to Okot's rescue. "C'mon, lads," he said, when about half the bales had been unloaded. "It's past suppertime, and we won't be holdin' the ship up none if this ain't finished 'till the mornin'." He called out to the man on board, who closed the hatch in the deck and came ashore with the others.

In a moment all was silent. Okot peered out cautiously. No one. He slipped out from behind the wagon wheel and ran silently down the gangplank. The schooner was much smaller than the slave ship that had brought him from Africa, but it was still a huge vessel. Sails were piled on the wooden decks, and smaller rowing boats were turned upside down and lashed to the gunwales. *Lots of places to hide,* Okot thought.

Just then the door to the wheelhouse swung open. The yellow shaft from a lantern lit the deck. Okot ducked behind the base of a mast. "Here, puss, puss, puss," someone called. "Dinnertime, you lazy brute." An arm from inside flung a handful of scraps onto the deck, and the door slammed shut again.

Okot crouched down and snatched up the pieces— nothing but a few small chunks of gristly beef, but he squatted behind the mast and ate the lot. After nearly three days without food, anything tasted good. He chewed and sucked for ages on the gristle, wishing he had more.

The cat appeared from under one of the rowboats and mewed indignantly. Okot hoped the man inside would throw out some more scraps, but nothing happened and finally the lantern was put out. Okot wormed his way under the rowboat where the cat had been sleeping and wrapped himself up in his blanket. He dreamed he was back on the slave ship, and woke up sweating with fear to hear the wind in the rigging and the water slapping against the sides of the ship. But he was warm and comfortable, and the cat was snuggled up against his chest, licking his fingers. "Sorry I ate your dinner," he whispered softly.

He put his arm around the furry creature, and this time slept dreamlessly and deeply.

The heavy tramping of feet up and down the gangplank woke Okot long before dawn. The men were loading the rest of the cotton bales. Not long after, with a lot of shouting, the squeaking of winches and thwacking of ropes, they set sail. Okot lay listening to the noises that he remembered from the slave traders' ship in the months it had taken to sail from Africa to the New World. That ship had been taking him into slavery. This ship was taking him to freedom. His heart beat high and fast.

"A fair wind today, eh Cap'n?"

The voice came so close and loud that Okot froze in terror. But he was still safely hidden. He could just see the boots of the men under the edge of the rowboat.

"Aye, a fair reaching breeze all the way across, I reckon," the other said. "Should make port in time to unload before dark."

But what port? Okot wondered. Maybe it didn't matter, as long as it was in Upper Canada. But how could he get ashore in daylight without being seen? One thing he knew, he did not want to spend another night here, with nothing to eat or drink. What would happen, he wondered, if the ship's crew found him? Would they let him go?

But the other slaves at the Abbots' plantation had talked about there being a bounty on escaped slaves. "That mean a white man get money if'n he catch another man's runaway slave," Elisha had told Okot. "Can't trust no white man not to turn you in."

I've got to be extra careful now, Okot told himself. The thought of being caught and sent back after getting this close to Upper Canada made him feel sick and shivery.

"No one's gonna catch me!" he muttered furiously, gritting his teeth. Somehow he would find a way to get off the ship without being seen.

Hours later, Okot was so hot and thirsty that he thought he couldn't stand it any more. It must have been late afternoon, because the sun's rays were slanting in under his hiding place. For some time he had heard nothing but the creaking of the spars and splashing of water. Cautiously he squirmed out between the rowboat and the gunwales. Just ahead of him, half hidden by a huge sail bag, a sailor was standing at the wheel. He had his back to Okot.

Peering out across the water, Okot saw a smudge of land in the distance. It got clearer every minute until he could see that it was a long spit jutting out into the lake. But the ship was turning to run along the shoreline. Okot's heart pounded in his ears. The spit of land was heavily wooded. Further down the main shore he saw smoke from many chimneys, and the masts of ships rising above the horizon. *Time to jump,* he thought.

It took all his courage to creep back to the stern railing. Silently he lowered himself over the side. The water rushed past much faster than he had expected. Taking a deep breath, he let go and dropped into the lake.

Okot gasped in shock as the dark water closed over his head, but he stayed under as long as he could. When he had to come up for air the ship was already well ahead of him. He had done it!

The ship had disappeared and the sun was almost set by the time Okot swam close enough to the shore to see the leaves on the trees and smell the rich soil of the forest. He was so tired that when his feet touched the rough shingle beach he just lay there, half in and half out of the water. He didn't move until he felt a little creature nibbling at his arm. It was like a huge spider, but with a hard shell. When he moved it scuttled away and disappeared down a tiny hole in the sandy soil.

I made it! Okot thought. *I'm in Upper Canada! I'm free!* He dragged himself to his knees and looked around. The forest was thick and dark, starting only a few feet away from the shore. For a minute Okot was afraid. He was completely alone. He almost wished he were back in his cabin with Mandy and Elisha, with salt herring and corn mush for supper, and his straw mattress to sleep on.

But only for a moment. "I'm free!" he said, this time out loud. It was strange to hear his voice again, after so many weeks of silence. He got to his feet and kept saying it as he walked up on the grassy shore. "I'm free!" He saw a thicket of bushes, heavy with bright red currants, and picked a handful of the fruit. He began to feel better. He didn't have his blanket any more, and his clothes were soaking wet. But he was in Upper Canada. Everything was going to be all right.

Chapter 8

Bear Claws and Blue Jays

Chipagawana didn't know how long he had been lying alone in the woods. He was sick with fever and pain from the wounds in his leg. The days and nights all ran together. Sometimes he imagined that the hunting party had found him, and he saw his father's face. But when he blinked away the sweat from his eyes the face always vanished.

Once he woke to feel Proudfoot nuzzling his face. He was afraid he was imagining things again, but he wasn't. His faithful friend had come back. Later, Chipagawana saw that his horse was badly hurt too. Proudfoot's flank was torn open from the bear's claws.

There was nothing Chipagawana could do to help. He couldn't even help himself.

In all that time, Chipagawana did not hear or see another soul. He began to wish someone would find him. Anyone. Even someone from another tribe. Nothing could be worse than lying alone like this, dying of pain and thirst.

Then, one morning, he heard something. *Maybe it's just the wind,* he thought. *Or a rabbit or a chipmunk rustling the leaves.* But his heart raced anyway. Then he heard it again. This time he was sure. Someone was creeping up on him. One of his people? Or an enemy?

He gave one of the low birdcalls that his hunting party would know. There was no response. Chipagawana felt fear go down his body like cold rain. An ant walked across his face but he didn't move.

Proudfoot sensed something too. His eyes rolled until they were nearly all white, and he pranced nervously.

Using every bit of strength he had, Chipagawana picked up his bow and pushed himself to his feet. Leaning against a tree, he fitted an arrow on the string and drew his bow taut.

Okot sensed something, or someone, in the woods ahead of him. The hair prickled on the back of his neck.

In the days since he'd swum ashore Okot had seen only two men. They were white men, and they had been sitting by a campfire in a small glade, roasting curious pieces of meat for their lunch on long sharp sticks. Okot had heard them talking and laughing, but they spoke a different language, not English, so he couldn't understand them.

The meat, he discovered, was from a snake. When the men left their camp, Okot had found the remains of the creature, with its thick dappled skin and a curious ridged rattle at the end. It must have been as long as his arm, and there was still a lot of meat left, so Okot finished skinning it. He risked fanning the embers the men had left into a little fire, and roasted the snake for his supper. It tasted like the chicken he had sometimes been given for lunch when he was working in Mrs. Abbot's garden. It was a good meal, hot and satisfying, and he slept well that night.

He discovered in the next few days that there were many of these rattling snakes in the woods of Upper Canada. By watching and waiting, crouched dead still with his knife ready, he trained his sharp eyes to see them slithering silently in the dead leaves of the forest floor. The first time a flicker of sunlight picked one up in the dank undergrowth Okot struck it with a lightning blow. If he'd had a good hunting knife he would have whacked it cleanly in half, but his little kitchen knife only went halfway through the thick hide. The snake writhed and whipped around before it died, and Okot had to leap back to avoid being bitten. But he couldn't help letting out a whoop of triumph.

Okot had seen how the strange rattle buzzed and made the little forest creatures petrified with fear. He cut the rattle off the first snake he killed and left it to dry in the sun while he was sleeping. He had carried it ever since as a trophy.

Now, sensing the presence of something hiding in the woods, Okot stealthily pulled the dried rattle from his pocket. If it was a person, it must be someone who was as afraid of being seen as Okot was. He would find out.

Okot shook the rattle. There was a quick intake of breath up ahead. Now he *knew*. It was a person. He stuck the rattle back in his pocket and pressed himself flat against a thick pine trunk. He was reaching for his knife when, out of nowhere, a boy his age appeared. A boy like no one he had ever seen. He was not black, but he wasn't white either. His dusky skin was pale with sickness except where a ragged gash, just beginning to heal, ran purple and red across his forehead and cheek. His straight black hair was wet with sweat. He leaned hard against a young oak, swaying as though he might fall.

A loud snort broke the silence. Okot nearly jumped out of his skin. A horse stood just beyond the sick boy, half-hidden by a bush. Its nostrils were flared and it stamped the ground impatiently.

Okot's wide eyes returned to the strange boy. He held his bow fully drawn, and the nocked arrow, with a wicked point, was aimed at Okot's side.

Slowly, Okot put his hands up over his head.

Chipagawana had been ready for anything except a boy his own age. A boy as black as a new moon sky, tall and narrow as a sapling. His hair was black too, like Chipagawana's, but not straight and shiny. It curled tightly to his head like moss on a rock. He was not carrying a bow or lance, but he might have a knife. Chipagawana wasn't taking any chances.

The two stared at each other for several minutes. But finally Chipagawana couldn't stand any more. His wounded leg throbbed unbearably and he was afraid he would fall over. Slowly he relaxed his bow arm and let the arrow point to the ground.

Okot saw the other boy sway. *He's sick, or hurt,* he thought. *Maybe he's as scared of me as I am of him.* He breathed deeply and let his hands fall to his sides.

Chipagawana's face was wet with sweat. His buckskin shirt was damp and stained. His lips were cracked and dry. His eyes darted all around them. After a minute he said in a croaky kind of voice like a frog, "There is a rattlesnake near here. I heard it."

Of course, Chipagawana spoke in his own Onondaga language. Okot had no idea what he was saying. He shrugged his shoulders and shook his head to show that he didn't understand.

Chipagawana licked his dry lips. Then he made a buzzing noise, somewhere back in his throat. With his free hand he made a weaving motion, like a snake.

The message was as clear as English. This boy was worried about the rattle he'd heard! Okot grinned. Moving slowly, he took out the rattle and shook it. All around them the birds stopped singing.

The other boy's eyes opened wide. "Aiee," he said softly. At last he lowered himself down to sit on his bed of cedar branches. Okot sat on the forest floor beside him with his legs sticking straight out in front, African style.

Chipagawana spoke first, still in his own language. "I am Chipagawana, of the Onondaga tribe," he said. "What tribe are you from?"

The words sounded as strange to Okot as English had when he first heard it from the slave raiders. He shook his head, and shrugged his shoulders again. He spoke back in English. "My name is Okot Deng. This country is new to me. Are we in Upper Canada?"

The other boy didn't answer. But he tilted his head slightly, as though he recognized some of Okot's words. He let the bow and arrow rest on his knees.

Okot remembered how the Africans and white men had tried to communicate their names when none of them spoke the same language. He pointed to himself and said, "Me, Okot."

Chipagawana thumped himself on the chest with his fist. "Me, Chipagawana."

Okot pointed at him. "You, Chipa—Chipawag—Chipnawa—" He gave up. He said, "I don't know how to say that."

Chipagawana nodded gravely. He knew that many white men had trouble understanding his language. It must be the same for this black person. He pointed and said, "You, Okot?" Okot nodded. He pointed to the flask slung over Okot's shoulder. "Water?"

Okot frowned. He had only a little left. But this boy looked so sick. He pulled out the cork and offered the bottle.

Chipagawana's mouth was so dry he could hardly swallow. But he still sniffed the strange flask carefully before he drank. The cool water was the best thing he had ever tasted. He drank so fast that it dribbled down his chin and neck. When he was finished, he handed back the bottle to Okot with a deep sigh. "Thanks you," he said, very seriously, in English.

"We need more," Okot said, holding the flask upside down.

Chipagawana knew there must be a spring or stream nearby, because Proudfoot limped away every day through the woods and came back with a dripping muzzle. Chipagawana pointed in that direction.

Okot could see that a new trail had been pounded through the trees where the horse's hooves had packed down the pine needles and dead leaves. He nodded and stood up. He moved so quickly, like a shadow, that Chipagawana snatched up his bow again. Okot stopped and flattened himself against a tree. Chipagawana relaxed. But he was still breathing hard. His face was like stone. Okot walked away slowly, holding his hands in front of him the way he had been taught as a slave. *I'll have to be more careful,* he thought, *or he'll shoot me even if I did give him my water.*

The stream ran swift and silver-bright through the middle of a wide grassy clearing, splashing over mossy rocks near the top and then disappearing in deep blue shadows back into the forest. The clearing was only about two hundred steps away through the woods, but even that was too far for the wounded boy to have walked on his own. Okot knelt on the springy bank, cupping his hands and drinking the cool clear water. He filled his flask and then rocked back on his heels to look around him.

The sun shone high overhead in a clear blue sky. Birds twittered in the trees, darting from branch to branch. There was a tangle of brambles just like those in the berry patch back at the plantation. Okot trotted over to them and found they were heavy with raspberries. He picked a handful and ate them.

The clearing reminded him of the grassy fields by the river Lol. He almost expected to see smoke rising from a Dinka family's fire. With a sigh Okot returned down the trail through the trees. He didn't know what was going to happen, now that he had met this strange boy with the arrows. But he was still happy to be with someone after all the time on his own.

Chipagawana had his bow and arrow at the ready again. But when Okot returned, he dropped them and reached eagerly for the water. When he had drunk his fill, he said again, "Thanks you." Then he pointed to his leg. "Bear hurt me."

Okot looked at the ugly wounds. He couldn't imagine how much it must have hurt to be clawed by a bear. "You're brave," he said admiringly.

Chipagawana almost smiled. "Aiee!" he cried, pointing to his chest. "Yes. Onondaga brave."

Okot sat down again, closer than before. The two looked at each other for a long time. They sat so quietly that a bird flew by and perched on a branch right above Chipagawana's head. He looked up at it and thought, *This blue jay is different from the other birds in the forest. It makes a loud shout to warn other birds and animals when there is danger around. But now it is quiet. It must feel safe. There must be no danger here.*

Okot had not seen such a beautiful bird since he left Africa. The brilliant blue feathers and crest stood out clearly against the green needles of the pine tree. *It must feel very safe,* he thought, *to rest there where it is so easy to see. I guess I'm safe with this strange boy too.*

In a minute, another of the blue birds lighted next to the first. The branch swayed under their weight as they chattered to each other. They reminded Okot of the women who came to visit Mrs. Abbot on the plantation, dressed in their bright dresses and gossiping while they drank their tea.

Then Proudfoot nudged Chipagawana's back, and the birds flew away.

In the sudden silence, Okot's stomach grumbled. It sounded like rumbling thunder, and both boys grinned.

It might be a long time before they trusted each other. But at least they weren't alone anymore.

Chapter 9

Land of the Great Spirit

Chipagawana rubbed his stomach. They had no problem understanding each other with this sign language. "Food," he said. "Rabbit." He picked up his bow and arrow to show he would try to shoot one, but Okot wondered if he just felt better holding his bow. He shrugged his shoulders. He did not expect Chipana-what's-his-name to let him use the bow. And *he* certainly couldn't hunt anything himself.

I'd have a better chance hitting a rabbit with a stone, Okot thought. He supposed they would have to eat nothing but berries and nuts again. He raised his hand to Chipagawana, pointing to his mouth and then toward the stream. "Berries there," he said. He didn't know if the other boy understood, but he went back down the path.

Back at the clearing, Okot plucked a handful of wide leaves from an oak tree. He held up the front of his shirt to use as a basket and lined it with the leaves. His eyes swept the grassy area as he picked the raspberries. There were rock outcroppings all over in these woods, and the clearing was no exception. Okot saw several places that would make good shelters. And there was the stream. There were berries to eat—he could see currant bushes too, and he thought there would be blackberries on some of the brambles. There were oak trees, and hazel bushes heavy with nuts. And there was good grazing for the horse. It was an ideal place to camp. He licked the berry juice from his fingers and thought about how to communicate this to Chipawa-whosis.

Meanwhile, Chipagawana sat still as a stone, an arrow ready on the string. He had seen many rabbits and squirrels run past him but he had been too sick to care about eating. Now it was different. The long drink of fresh cold water had made him realize he was starving.

He didn't have long to wait. A rabbit hopped into view, intent on some tender green shoots pushing up through the carpet of brown pine needles and decaying leaves. Chipagawana took aim and let his arrow fly. The rabbit fell over without a sound.

Okot returned just in time to hear the zing of the bowstring. An arrow zipped past his face. He stopped, stiff and still, his eyes opened wide. He only kept a hold on his load of berries because his hands were clenched so tightly on his shirt.

Slowly he turned in the direction the arrow had flown, and saw it sticking out of the dead rabbit. He laughed shakily. Putting down the berries on their nest of leaves, he picked up the rabbit and carried it back. "Good shot," he said. "You could be a Dinka tribesman." He pulled out the arrow and cleaned the blood off by rubbing it in the dried pine needles.

Chipagawana frowned, not understanding. He reached down to pull his knife from the sheath on his leg, and began to skin the rabbit.

Okot's eyes narrowed. He licked his lips nervously, and then took out his own knife to sharpen it against a stone. It was puny next to the other boy's, but he wanted to show that he could look after himself too.

Their eyes met. Then Chipagawana pursed his lips and made a chattering noise like the blue jays. Startled, Okot grinned. "Okay," he said. "It's all right now."

Chipagawana nodded, and went back to cleaning the rabbit.

"Your name," Okot said. He tried again. "Chipna— Chipwag—" He shook his head. "I can't say it. Can I call you Chip?"

Chipagawana frowned. "Can call? What means?"

Okot pointed to his chest. "Me, Okot." He pointed at Chipagawana. "You Chip."

"Me, Chipagawana."

Okot shook his head. They would have to work it out somehow.

Chip finished skinning the rabbit and Okot took it to the stream to gut it. He looked around the clearing while he washed the meat, trying to pick out the best place to camp. By the time he returned Chip had sharpened the end of a sturdy green branch for a skewer. Okot threaded the cleaned rabbit onto it. Then he looked around through the trees until he found two sturdy sticks that each had a Y-shaped crotch. These would hold the ends of the skewer, so the rabbit could hang over a fire to roast. Now, all they needed was a fire.

Chip sharpened the sticks and stuck them in the ground. He groaned with pain at the effort. When they had hung the rabbit he said, "Now, fire." Okot helped him make a heap of dried grass, leaves, pine needles, and twigs. He cut a few lumps of resin from one of the pine trees to add to the fire. He had learned that they were easy to light, and burned hot and fast. Chip nodded yes. He knew it too. Then, just as Okot was about to take the flint and steel from his pouch, Chip began to do a strange thing.

He put a piece of flat, dry wood next to the pile of tinder. Then he twisted a stick into his bowstring. He put one end of the stick on the little piece of dry wood, and began to push his bow back and forth like a saw, holding the stick down with a stone. The stick spun in a blur.

Okot was fascinated. He could smell the wood growing hot. Then smoke started coming up. Chip blew gently on the dry grass, still twirling the stick. There was a little puff of smoke as the grass began to smolder. Chip quickly dropped his bow and pushed more grass onto the fire. He added dry leaves, and then the twigs, one at a time, until the fire was crackling with little flames.

Quickly Okot gathered some larger branches, and they fed them one at a time into the fire. When there was a good bed of hot coals, they hung the rabbit over the fire. Almost immediately the smell of roasting meat made their stomachs rumble. They ate some of the wild raspberries, and the last of Okot's walnuts.

They listened for a while to the crackling of the fire. Okot was nearly crazy with hunger, so to distract himself he said, "What's the name of this place?"

"This place?" Chip frowned. "This—trees?"

"Yes, these woods," Okot said, waving his arms around. "What name?"

"Is land of Great Spirit."

Okot thought hard. Mandy had talked about a Spirit, too. He said, "Is the Great Spirit God?"

"God?" Chip shook his head, not understanding. "All land belong to Great Spirit. White men fight for land. Great Spirit angry. Send sickness. Send death."

"What about black men? Slaves?"

Chip crinkled his forehead. "Slaves? What is slaves?"

"Is this Upper Canada?" Okot asked again.

This time Chip nodded. "White men call Great Spirit land Upper Canada."

Okot felt as though a great load had dropped off his back. He felt hungrier than he had in months, but this was a different kind of hunger. There was no sickness left inside him. He was free, and no one could send him back.

They ate the rabbit with the rest of the wild raspberries. The sweet berry juice ran down their chins, and they burned their tongues on the hot roasted meat, but it didn't matter. They shared Okot's water bottle, taking long cool drinks. When it was empty, he went back to the stream to fill it up. They ate until all the meat was gone, and then they chewed on the bones. Okot thought it was the best feeling in the world, being so full of good food, with no overseer casting his shadow over him, and no one to tell him what to do.

The sun had climbed high overhead while they made their lunch, and now it was moving lower in the sky. Okot fetched more water so they could wash their sticky hands and faces. Then he said, "We could make a good camp by the water. Better'n here. I can help you there." He made signs of getting up, pointing to Chip's bed of evergreen boughs, and then to the path to the stream. "Much better. We should go now, before dark."

Okot knew Chip understood him by the way his eyes flashed back and forth wherever Okot pointed. But Okot would have to help him walk. And Chip would have to trust Okot to take his bow and arrow.

There was a long, long silence. At last Chip dropped his eyes to the ground. "Not go," he said. "Not move."

The food and water had helped Chip a lot. But his gouged leg was badly infected, red hot and swollen. He knew he could help it by making medicine from a birch tree, but he couldn't see any in the woods around him. And he couldn't explain what he needed to Okot.

The sun went down and the evening grew cool. Chip curled up on his bed under the pine tree, trying to make his throbbing leg comfortable. Okot climbed up a maple tree a little distance away. He settled himself to sleep, but for a long time he and Chip peered at each other through the darkness. Both of them wondered what would happen in the morning.

Chapter 10

The Ways of the Forest

In the morning Okot fell out of his tree.

He was dreaming that the hounds from the plantation were chasing him again. He rolled in his sleep and then let out a startled cry, grabbing at a branch and trying to hang on. His feet slipped and he slithered down the tree trunk, landing with a thud on his backside.

He jumped up quickly, rubbing the seat of his breeches, and looked to see if Chip was still sleeping. He'd have hated Chip to see him fall.

Chip looked at Okot through half-closed eyes. He pretended to be asleep, but he was having a hard time not laughing. When Okot went off into the trees to go to the toilet, Chip pushed off his covering of pine boughs and sat up.

Fresh jabs of pain shot though his leg. It was now so swollen that even his torn legging was too tight. He took out his knife and slit the buckskin. That helped a bit, but now there was nothing to protect the wounds.

Would his leg heal so that he could travel back to his own people? Would Proudfoot be strong enough to carry him? And what about Okot? What was this strange black person doing here, alone in the woods? Where was he going to?

Chip was sitting hunched over, thinking of these things, when Okot came back. Suddenly Chip lifted a finger to his mouth, signaling Okot to be quiet.

Okot stopped dead. Chip pointed through the trees to his right. Okot saw a great black bear on the other side of the tree where he had slept. A moment later they saw it had two cubs with it. *There must be a great many of these creatures in the New World,* Okot thought.

Chip struggled to stand up. Quietly he nocked an arrow and drew his bow taut. He would be ready if it charged them—even though he knew it would be hopeless. He couldn't kill it before it mauled them.

It seemed like hours that they waited and watched as the bears foraged through the undergrowth. Okot remembered the time he had been pinned in the cave in the thunderstorm just after his escape. He thought of Chip's leg and the horse's flank, and his heart thudded in his thin chest. He wondered if bears charged the way lions sometimes did in Africa. They didn't like to be disturbed when they were eating.

The bear cubs rolled on the ground, scratching themselves against the tree roots and wrestling with each other. They looked like giant kittens playing in the sunlight. It was hard to imagine that they were really dangerous.

Suddenly the mother bear lifted its nose in the air. The breeze had shifted and it smelled Okot and Chip. It let out a low growl. The cubs scrabbled to her side.

Chip whistled. It was a high, shrill, ear-blasting sound. His horse snorted and answered with a wild whinny. The bear shook its great head as though something was hurting it. Chip kept on whistling. The bear reared up on its hind legs and batted at the air with its paws. The terrified horse screamed, but could not run because of his lame side.

Okot started toward Chip but the Indian boy stopped him with a small sharp hand signal. "Not move. Bear no see."

It was true. The breeze had swung around again. The bear dropped to all fours and sniffed the air. It seemed puzzled. Chip and Okot were still as stones, scarcely breathing. Then, with a snort, the bear and its cubs waddled off into the forest.

After a few more long minutes of silence the boys smiled at each other. Okot helped Chip sit down again. Chip even let him take his bow and arrow and lay them down beside him.

Okot pointed to the infected gouges on Chip's leg. "Your leg is very sick."

"Yes. It need medicine. Not here."

"Chip," Okot said, "we have to go to the stream. Then you can wash it. That gonna be better. I can take you."

"My name Chipagawana."

"I know. I just can't say it. You gotta be Chip till I learns your language. Are we gonna go to the water?"

Finally Chip nodded. He was too sick to object any more. So Okot slung the bow and quiver of arrows across his shoulder and helped Chip stand again. He took as much of the other boy's weight as he could. Chip groaned. He held tightly to Okot's waist and they made their way slowly to the clearing.

Okot thought they would never reach the stream. He had almost begun to think that he had only imagined it when they finally reached the wide clearing. Chip was sweating all over from pain and exhaustion. Okot helped him down to the water. They waded in and Chip sat down.

At first the cold water going over the wound made it hurt even more. But in a few minutes it began to feel better as the clean water washed away the dirt and blood.

Okot felt better when he saw the look of pain leave Chip's face. His stomach growled with hunger and he wished that they had some of the roasted rabbit left. He picked more raspberries and shared them with Chip, crouching at the edge of the water. Then he went back into the woods to pick up his blanket and the sticks they had used for skewering and cooking the rabbit. He hoped they would need them again.

When Chip had had enough of the water, Okot helped him out, and together they chose a place to camp. One of the rocky outcroppings had a broad overhang that made a deep sheltered place underneath. A green thorny mass of wild brambles grew all over the rocks. The entrance was partly hidden on one side by a large boulder, and a maple sapling had pushed its way up through the rocky soil on the other side. It overlooked the stream, and if they built a fire it wouldn't be visible from the woods that surrounded the clearing. They could see that animals had used it in the past, because the grasses had been worn down into a kind of hollow nest, but it was clean and dry. In fact, it was nicer in every way than the cabin Okot had shared with Mandy and Elisha.

"Aiee!" Chip said softly, when they found it. "Great Spirit smile on us. Make healing place." He placed his bow and quiver of arrows carefully by the entrance, as though sealing a pact with his Great Spirit. The boys grinned at each other shyly. All at once, even though Chip and his horse were so badly hurt, and even though Okot didn't have a real home or any family, they both felt as though they were out on a great adventure. They had shelter and water. They could make fire, and they could hunt for food.

Okot went off to the woods to cut down fresh evergreen branches. They laid them out against the back wall of the shelter, making a bed big enough for both of them, and covered it with huge tufts of dried grasses from the forest's edge. Their new home was finished. They looked over their work with satisfaction, and then sat outside on the grass in the warm sun.

Chip's horse had followed them back to the clearing and was standing switching his tail and stamping his hooves to rid himself of the flies that swarmed about his wounds. His ribs showed through his staring coat, yet he barely nibbled at the tender fresh grass by the stream. Chip pointed to him. "My horse. Proudfoot. Him hurted too." Then he asked Okot, "How many moons you be lost?"

"I been runnin' almost two moons," Okot said. "I was a slave. I was runnin' to get to Upper Canada, away from white men."

"Is white men here. Many." Chip thought Okot was looking for white men. "What mean 'slave'?"

Okot didn't know how to explain. He took off his shirt and showed Chip the scars on his back. "White men's always whippin' black men." Chip frowned, not understanding. Okot broke a thin branch from one of the bushes by the stream and whacked it with all his strength against the ground. "This be whippin'," he said. "White men hates us. So I's run away."

"Here in Great Spirit land is many white men. Many Haudenosaunee fight with white men."

Haudenosaunee? Okot grunted. That was even harder than Chipa-whatever-his-name-was. Okot guessed it must be the name of Chip's tribe. "Chip, how many moons have you been runnin' away?" he asked.

"My name Chipagawana. Not run. No whip. We hunt, from my village. Thunder Arm. My father. This days we ride from village." He held up nine fingers. "Hunt deer. Hunt bear. Good food. Good fur."

Slowly, with much sign language, he told Okot the story of how the bear charged him on Proudfoot, and how he had lost consciousness and fallen off in the forest. He had no idea how far they had come. It must have been a long way, since no one from the hunting party had been able to find him.

"You know they lookin' for you?" Okot asked.

"Maybe. Maybe go back to village. Ohsweken. I must find village now. When leg not sick no more. When Proudfoot…when he not sick. We go find my village."

"We." Chip had said "we." Okot felt a warm glow in his belly. This strange boy might take him back to his tribe. Would they be friendly? It seemed a better choice than trying to live in a white man's village, even if he was in the free North.

Chip looked up at the sun burning high in the sky and rubbed his stomach. "Hunger time. We catch fish now. Make good fire."

Okot thought back to fishing with his friends on the Lol River. They always went early, in their mango tree canoes, and roasted their catch over hot coals in the midday sunshine. Okot's mouth watered. But how were they going to catch fish here? Chip made it sound like a simple thing.

It was simple. Chip asked Okot to help him down to the stream again. His wounds looked less sore and red after his soak in the water, but he couldn't put any weight on the leg. He waded into the stream, leaning on Okot and holding an arrow ready on his bow. They stood quietly for a few minutes. Okot's legs grew stiff with cold.

Then he heard the zing of an arrow. The water exploded. A fish leaped and thrashed with the arrow in its side. Okot pulled it out of the water by its gills. He had never seen such a fish. It was as long as his forearm and it flashed in the sunlight with all the colors of the sky at sunset.

Back on the bank of the stream, Chip smacked the head of the fish with a stone to kill it. When it stopped flopping about he pulled it off the arrow and took out his knife.

"This be trout," he said, as he sharpened his knife on a stone. "It has storm-sky colors—" He frowned, trying to find the right word. He made a big arc with his hands, waving his knife in the air. Okot jumped back, his heart thumping. But Chip didn't notice. He was too busy trying to explain about the fish colors. "How you call this trout? Sky color. Great Spirit smile on us." He dropped his arms and went back to sharpening his knife.

Okot took a deep breath. He knelt next to Chip and looked at the colors on the fish. Storm sky? "Rainbow!" he cried, remembering the sky over the fields at the Abbot plantation after the big storm. Okot had asked Mandy the English name for the beautiful colored bow in the sky that reminded him so much of the savannah around Nyamlel during the long rains. "A rainbow," she'd said. "It's a promise from God."

"Rain bow." Chip tried it out, like two words. "Yes," he grinned. "Rain bow trout. Many many rain bow trout in Onondaga rivers. Is gift from Great Spirit."

Okot thought about that as he gathered leaves and twigs to make a fire. A promise from Mandy's God? A gift from the Great Spirit of Chip's tribe? Were they the same? He shook his head until it hurt. Would he ever understand it?

Chapter 11

The Coming of White Man

Chip finished sharpening his knife and began to clean the trout. He placed it on its side on a flat rock and held it firmly by the top gill. He showed Okot the soft triangle between the fish's mouth and gill and throat. "Cut here," he said, using the point of his knife. "All back along fish belly. Not too deep. Just under skin." He sliced the trout open in one long quick cut, back to the tail. "Then pull—pull this." He didn't know any English word for the fish's insides.

But Okot did, because of what Elisha and the other slaves had taught him. He said, "Them's guts, boy," just the way Elisha had first said it.

Chip shrugged. English was certainly a strange language. "So," he said. "Pull them's gutsboy back to front." He grasped the trout's insides and pulled them out, to the throat. "Then cut." He sliced them out, at the throat, where he had made his first cut. "Be care," he said, pointing to a small yellow sac. "Not cut. Make ugly taste. Like white man medicine." He made a face to show what he meant, and threw the guts in the stream. "Now." He spread the cleaned fish open and showed Okot a black line running along the backbone. "More them's gutsboy." He put down his knife and pushed his thumbnail all along the black line, pushing it out. Then he rinsed the fish in the stream. "Now make good food."

Okot fetched some twigs and dried leaves for the fire. He was too hungry to wait all the time it would take Chip to start the fire with his bow and stick again, so he reached into his leather pouch and pulled out his flint and steel.

Chip grinned, and took a flint from his own deerskin pouch. Then they both laughed. Chip had just been showing off before. He'd wanted this strange black person to see that he was skilled in the ways of an Indian brave.

They soon had a good fire going on the bank of the stream. Chip pushed the flat stone into the fire, and when it was hot he put the whole trout on top. Okot had found a great tangle of wild grape vines further upstream, and while the trout roasted he went off to pick some of the fruit.

Chip turned the fish once with his knife, and when it was done they ate it right there in the sunshine by the stream. The flesh was a little dry, but rosy pink like a summer evening, and the skin was crisp and smoky from the fire.

"It's good," Okot told Chip. "Very different from the fish from the Lol River."

"What Lol?" Chip asked with his mouth full.

"The river by my village in Africa. My home."

They didn't say anything else for a while. They were both thinking about home. Then Okot broke the silence. "I wish we had salt," he said.

Chip had no trouble understanding "salt." Thunder Arm sometimes came back from the trading post with sacks of salt. "Aiee," he murmured, "Salt be good." They both licked their fingers thoughtfully. Thinking about salt was better than thinking about their faraway villages.

After the fish they ate the grapes, which were still a bit hard and sour but cool on their burned tongues. Then Chip wanted to look at Proudfoot's wounds. The scruffy half-wild paint wouldn't let Okot near, so Chip whistled for him. He came slowly, dragging the hind leg on his wounded side, and stood with his head hanging down. His coat was rough and sweaty. "Him need stream too," Chip said.

So they spent the afternoon in the water. Chip sat in the shallows near the bank. Okot held Proudfoot in the stronger current in the middle, where the water was deep enough to come nearly to the horse's withers.

It wasn't long before Okot was cold and uncomfortable. He had often stood for hours in the Lol River, leaning on his spear and looking for fish. But that water was warm, and the African sun hot. And besides, there were always many birds to watch wheeling and soaring in the skies, and butterflies flitted everywhere in the grasslands. Here scarcely anything moved or made a sound. He cheered himself up by thinking how funny they would look if anyone could see them. Especially Chip, who sat up to his waist in the water, with his bow and arrow ready to shoot anything that moved. He never relaxed.

I guess, Okot thought, *that's the way Indians are. Maybe that's why they're not slaves.*

They were so still and quiet that the timid creatures of the woods began to appear in the clearing. Squirrels scampered along their own invisible paths, their cheeks bulging with nuts. A rabbit came to nibble the freshly sprouting grasses by the water. Okot was just wondering why Chip didn't shoot it for their supper when he heard the twang of the bow and the whoosh of an arrow.

This time Chip had shot a bird. "Aiee!" he hollered, breaking the long silence. The startled rabbit bounded away. Proudfoot threw up his head and snorted.

Okot led Proudfoot out of the water and turned him loose. This time the shaggy little paint shook himself like any healthy horse and dropped his head to graze. Chip nodded with satisfaction. "Him get better too." He struggled to his feet and let Okot help him wade back to the bank.

The bird looked like the geese Okot had seen at the Abbots' plantation, except that this one was white only on the belly. Its feathers were different shades of brown, and there were black feathers on its back. It was enormous. With some effort Okot picked it up by the neck and carried it back to where Chip was sitting. "Is it a goose?" he asked.

"Goose?" Chip asked. He tried to remember what the white men called this bird. He shrugged. "Is good bird. Summer gift from Great Spirit. In winter, fly away." He began plucking feathers from the bird.

Okot remembered watching the slave women outside the kitchen of the plantation house, sitting in a circle chattering as they plucked six or seven geese for one of the many big dinners. He remembered the smell of the birds roasting, how it sometimes drifted down to the slave cabins on the breeze—how they all had craved a taste of something so delicious. He said to Chip, "I can do that, if you want."

Chip looked up, and then he frowned. Okot thought he was angry, but he pointed at the sky. Clouds had gathered in the west, blocking light from the setting sun. A cool breeze blew across the clearing. He said, "Is rain soon. No?"

"I guess so," Okot said.

"We make fire in shelter," Chip said. "For warm, and cooking."

So Okot made a new fire, just inside their rock shelter. This took a long time, because he had to build a base of stones for a fire pit. There were lots of small rocks around, but not many flat stones. He found some by the stream, but Chip shook his head.

"Not use," he said firmly. "Wet stone not good. Go boom!" Again he waved his arms and feathers flew all around him.

Okot went the other way, into the forest, and finally found enough flat stones to make a good circle, two layers deep. He heaped tinder in the pit and struck a spark to it with his flint and steel. Then he gathered wood, enough to build a good fire for roasting the goose, and more that he stacked just inside the shelter.

By this time Chip had finished plucking the goose. He looked tired and sick again. His face had a gray cast as though he had rubbed it with ashes. Okot said, "I'll clean the bird." He sharpened his knife on a stone as well as he could and then cut off the goose's neck. He held it over the water while he pulled out the guts and let them float away downstream.

Chip watched critically. Then he grinned. "Is good, Okot. Good squaw work."

Okot didn't know what "squaw work" was, but he was happy to see a smile on Chip's face. He helped him to the shelter and settled him down on their evergreen bed. Chip skewered the goose while Okot stirred the fire and added more wood.

Some of the branches made Chip very excited. "Good! Good!" he cried. "Where find?"

"Just there," Okot said, pointing upstream. He had gone to look at the clump of trees because they were so beautiful, not like any he had seen in Africa. They had bark the color of moonlight, which peeled off like dry skin when you pulled it.

"This birch," Chip said, taking out his knife. "This bark make good medicine. Good food." He took one of the branches and cut away until he came to a layer of fresh new bark underneath. He sliced off a few strips and immediately put one in his mouth to chew. He gave a piece to Okot.

Okot wrinkled his nose, but did as Chip said. To his surprise the bark was sweet and tender.

After a minute Chip spat out the chewed-up fibers. "Is good?"

"Very good," Okot said, taking another piece.

"Make good medicine for leg." Chip pointed to his wounds. He found a fat piece of birch wood in Okot's woodpile and cut a long wide thick piece of bark from it, working carefully so that it stayed in one piece. "This make cup," he explained. "For medicine drink."

While the goose was roasting, Chip made a kind of bowl out of his big piece of birch bark. First he cut the edges and folded them toward the middle. Then he made little holes with the point of his knife along the top edge. He wove a thin green birch twig through the holes to hold the sides together.

He grinned happily when he had finished. "Now wet good," he said, handing it to Okot. "Wet good in stream. Bring water." It took Okot three trips to the stream before he understood that Chip wanted the bark to soak in water for a while. Finally, Chip was happy with it. He put it, full of water, in the hot ashes near the edge of the fire. Then he added the rest of the sweet inner bark from the birch tree to the water.

Okot thought the bark cup would catch on fire, but it didn't. It got black on the outside, but the water boiled. After a while, Chip pushed the ashes away with his knife. When the sooty bowl was cool enough to pick up, he drank some of his strange medicine. Then he offered it to Okot.

The warm drink felt good in Okot's stomach. He said, "Do all your people know so much about the woods?"

"More. Much more," Chip said. "When I know more, I be brave."

Okot didn't understand that. He thought Chip was very brave already.

The fire crackled and spat as fat dripped from the roasting goose. Outside the rain began to fall. It pattered softly on the rocks and on the leaves of the trees. They could hear Proudfoot just outside the shelter, tearing up tufts of the thick fresh grass. "Is good," Chip said contentedly. "Proudfoot get better like me."

And then, Okot thought, *Chip will go back to his village. And what will happen to me? Will I fit in with Chip's people?* He said, "What's it like where you live?"

Chip told Okot about his people, the Hotahyonhne clan in the Onondaga tribe of the Haudenosaunee. Okot heard echoes of the tongue-twisting words in his head. They reminded him of the distant grunting of buffalo across the plains around Nyamlel. He wondered what they meant, but he didn't know how to ask, in case it offended Chip. So he just sat and listened as Chip described the longhouses his people lived in, covered with bark from the elm tree to keep them snug and dry. Chip talked about the meeting place in the middle of the longhouse, where the elders and chiefs of their Hotahyonhne clan planned wars and hunting parties, and taught the young men about the great history of the tribe. He told Okot about Thunder Arm, his father, who was so stern and proud, and who was starting to treat Chip like a warrior brave.

Over the next few days Okot learned much about Chip's tribe and his life in the village of Ohsweken. In turn, Okot told Chip about his months as a slave on the plantation, and his life back in Nyamlel. All their stories took hours to tell, and they often ended up howling with laughter at each other as they tried to communicate with pantomimes and sign language. But they had hours to spare, with nowhere to go and nothing to do except find enough to eat, and wait for Chip and Proudfoot to get well enough to travel.

By their fifth day together Chip's leg was so much better that he was able to walk between the shelter and the stream by himself. On that day he shot another goose. "This be wife of him we ate," Chip said. "This birds always come in two."

In the late afternoon, when the goose was roasting, Okot asked Chip about his family. So far, all of Chip's talk had been about wars and warriors, hunting and killing. Okot was getting tired of it.

Chip, sitting cross-legged on the evergreens, picked up a thin stick from the pile by the fire. He stripped off the bark, and then, with his knife, began to make shallow lengthwise cuts in it. Round and round he went, his knife making soft swishing sounds. "Is feather stick," he had explained to Okot the first night. "Make good fire." He carved the sticks whenever he was talking, and now there was quite a stack of them in the corner of the shelter. He finished one, and started another. "I have two brothers," he said, at last answering Okot. "Black Hawk and Swift Deer. They strong braves. And sister. Her name mean Dawn on Water. All braves in my tribe want marry her. They fight big when she make wife age." Chip's face darkened. "But she still small."

Dawn on Water, he said, had already learned how to prepare deer hide to make clothing, scraping and stretching it with her mother until it was soft and white as paper birch. All through the Moon of the Long Nights, the women of his longhouse snuggled warmly under thick bear rugs and sewed clothes from the deerskin, with needles made from the bones of wild partridges. When the shirts and leggings and dresses were finished, Dawn on Water decorated them with beads that Thunder Arm brought back from the white man's trading post.

Chip had smiled a little when he talked about his sister, but now his face grew hard again. He told Okot that there had been a great war, when the white men fought with each other. It was two years since the end of that war, but the warriors still talked about it around the campfire. "Those be bad times. Indian tribes fight with white men. Some with French. Some with English. Many killed. Tribes war at tribes. Great Spirit angry. No corn grow. White men bring sickness. Haudenosaunee medicine men not have strong magic for white men's sicknesses. Many die." Chip scowled, and started another feather stick.

"But now, white men not fight," he went on. "Onondaga got much food. Many deer in forest. Many fish in rivers. Harvest moon bring corn. Great Spirit smile on Haudenosaunee."

Then Chip told Okot about his grandfather, who hated the white men with their diseases, and their whisky that made even great Onondaga warriors into crazy men. He hated the white man's God, too. Their God came in a black book, and lived in strange buildings with crossed branches on the roof.

"They say Onondaga spirits no good. Say there no Great Spirit. They make Great Spirit angry. Onondaga kill white men who make Great Spirit angry. Then he smile on us again. Good harvest. Good hunting."

Okot didn't know what to say to that, so he said nothing. Chip's face was so fierce when he talked that it scared Okot. Outside, it was growing dark. There was a sudden burst of thunder. A great gust of icy wind blew into their shelter, making the fire billow with smoke. They were showered with hot ashes. Lightning slashed across the sky. Okot's eyes rolled with fear. Was Chip's Great Spirit angry with them? Was it because Okot had been thinking about Mandy's God? In his tribe in Africa, the Dinka priests knew all about the spirits. They knew what to do when the spirits were angry. But Okot didn't know. He shivered, wiping away the ashes from his arms and legs.

But Chip didn't seem worried. He just brushed himself off, and poked the roasting goose with a stick to see if it was ready to eat. In a few minutes the wind died down and the rain stopped. It had been nothing more than a quick summer storm.

Outside, they heard Proudfoot snort uneasily. Instantly Chip had his hand on his bow. Was it a bear? Or people? He and Okot stared at each other, wide-eyed. Cautiously they peered around the edge of the shelter.

Proudfoot was prancing nervously. They heard the soft thudding of hooves on the forest floor. A horse was coming. One? Or more? *The hunting party?* Chip wondered. But he shook his head. Thunder Arm and the braves would never ride so openly in unknown territory. It might be someone from another tribe. Or a white man.

All of Okot's fears came rushing back. *What if it's a white man?* he wondered. Was he really safe here, or would he have to run again?

Silently Chip slipped his knife out of its sheath. He handed it to Okot, and motioned for him to hide behind the boulder. Okot glided outside. Chip nocked an arrow and drew back his bow.

They waited, their eyes darting around the clearing, watching the dark forest. Then Okot saw a movement at the edge of the trees. Someone came riding out of the woods on a tall albino horse. He was not riding bareback, like the Indians. He sat in a deep saddle as though he had been born there, his back straight, his hands relaxed on the reins. He looked older than Okot and Chip, with strong broad shoulders like a man. White-blond hair covered his bare head in a mass of untidy curls, and even from a distance Okot and Chip could see the rider's searching blue eyes. He was white.

Chapter 12

Wolverine!

It was Paul, on his horse, Storm.

They burst into the clearing and he breathed a great sigh of relief when he saw the stream. He could camp here for the night. But then Storm nickered and surged forward, almost unseating Paul. He saw Proudfoot, standing still as a stone, ears pricked forward.

Paul reined in Storm and looked about uncertainly. This was an Indian's horse, an unclipped, sturdy little paint. *It has been injured—and by a bear*, Paul thought, looking at the great long claw marks along the horse's flank. *Had the Indian been hurt too? Killed maybe?* The horse looked thin and uncared for.

Then Paul smelled the smoke, and the wonderful aroma of roasting meat. The Indian must be camping here.

The horses sniffed each other, squealing and stamping the grass. Then they seemed to decide that two was better than one. They blew softly and nuzzled each other.

Paul searched the clearing in the twilight. He couldn't see the glow of a fire anywhere, but finally he saw the trickle of smoke coming from under a rocky overhang. And then he blinked. A tall, thin boy was standing in the shadows. Paul hadn't seen him before, because his skin was black. So black that he was almost invisible against the rocks. Only his eyes flashed white.

Paul knew there were black people in Africa. And black slaves, far to the south. His father and the settlers often talked about slavery, and the rebellions where slaves sometimes killed the white people who owned them. Many had escaped and come to Upper Canada, although Paul had never seen a black man himself.

Paul was so intent on staring at those white eyes in the darkness that he wasn't paying attention to Storm. Suddenly the horse shied wildly. This time Paul did come off. The fall knocked the wind out of him.

He tried to get to his feet, more embarrassed than afraid. But when he looked up, there was another boy there. An Indian boy, pointing a bow and arrow at his side.

They stayed that way, without moving, for several moments. Paul's heart pounded so hard he was sure the other boys could hear it. Then, slowly, the Indian lowered his bow. He and the black boy whispered to each other. "No hurt," the Indian said. "Only boy like us. No more people."

Okot was still frightened. The white boy was not as old as he had seemed in the saddle. *He must be with other men, grown men,* Okot thought. *He wouldn't be alone here in the forest. What if he knows about runaway slaves?* But the white boy looked pale and tired. Okot thought, *I bet he's as scared as we are.* Chip must be right, he decided at last. If there were others, they would be here by now. He nodded to Chip.

Slowly, Chip put his arm across his chest with his hand near his shoulder. It was a small sign of peace. But he kept his hand on his bow.

Paul put up his hand with the palm showing toward Chip and Okot. This was the sign of peace his father had taught him. The sign Brentwood was making the last time Paul saw him.

Chip pointed to the knife sheath strapped to Paul's belt. Paul hesitated, but he knew what his father would do. He prayed quickly to God to protect him. Then, slowly, he took the knife from the sheath and held it out with the handle pointing to the Indian boy.

Chip thought, *This boy is like the white man that Thunder Arm has met at the trading post. They say he trusts the white man's God.* Carefully, he too turned his palm out to Paul. Then he laid down his bow.

They all seemed to breathe again. Paul was going to lay down his knife, but Chip shook his head and said, "You not bad."

Paul grinned shakily. "No," he agreed. "I'm not bad. I'm lost. I was separated from my father. He's a preacher. We were traveling from Brant's Ford when we were attacked—" He stopped. *I'd better not say anything about the Indians ambushing me,* he thought. So he just added, "I've been trying to find him."

Okot said, "We're lost, too. Chip got lost from his father—"

"I only little lost!" Chip interrupted him. "I know land of my tribe. We go soon."

Just then, Paul's stomach growled like thunder. He didn't understand why the other two boys laughed so hard. "I haven't eaten for two days," he said. He wrinkled his nose. "I ate some berries. The wrong kind of berries." He clutched his stomach to show what he meant.

Chip said, "Make you go behind tree too many times?" Paul nodded, groaning as he remembered. "Come," Chip said, leading Paul into the shelter. "I have good medicine. Good meat too."

Paul grinned. "Thanks." But he looked back into the darkness. "First, I have to look after my horse."

Okot said, "I'll help."

They went out into the clearing together. Storm was standing like a statue, with the reins hanging to the ground. He nuzzled Paul in the chest, as if to apologize for his bad behavior. Paul laughed and rubbed the horse between the ears. "It's okay, Storm," he said. "It was my fault." He untied the girth and pulled off the heavy saddle. He had a pair of saddlebags too, and a bedroll, neatly wrapped in an oilskin. He hobbled the horse, and then took off the bridle. Storm immediately dropped his head to graze.

Okot carried the saddle, and Paul brought the other things with him as they walked back to the shelter. The smell of roast goose filled the air. Chip had boiled up some more of his birch-bark tea, and offered it to the white boy. "Good for bad berries," he said seriously.

Paul sniffed the hot liquid, and then drank it down. "It's good," he said. "I remember my father learning about this from Indians at the trading post."

The other two boys watched him silently. He began to feel nervous again. Had he done the right thing? Maybe he should leave now, before anything happened to him. But it was warm and snug in the shelter, with the comfort of the fire. He had been lonely, traveling and camping in the woods, thinking about his friend Freeman, and wondering what had happened to his father. He didn't want to leave.

Finally, he was so nervous that he started telling them his story. He told them everything he could think of, about his mother dying when he was born, about leaving England and sailing to the New World. He told them about his father being a Methodist preacher, and how he came to Upper Canada to preach the Gospel to the Indian people. "My name's Paul Brentwood," he added, at the end.

Okot understood a lot more of Paul's story than Chip did. But neither of them knew what a Methodist preacher or the Gospel was. One thing Okot did know was that Paul's English sounded just like the English of the sailors on the slave ship. And Paul came from the same place, the place called England. Okot wondered if this white boy had anything to do with the slave traders.

Finally, he said, "My name is Okot Deng."

Chip said, "I am Chipagawana."

Paul wished he could say the Indian names the way his father could. He frowned, trying to repeat the word.

Okot laughed. "I can't say his name either," he said. "I call him Chip."

Paul smiled in relief.

For once, Chip ignored this. He had been poking the roasting goose, and he said, "Is ready." He carved up the bird on a stone. Paul reached for one of his saddlebags and pulled out a little parcel. "Do you want some salt?" he asked.

Okot and Chip grinned at each other. "Aiee!" Chip shouted, licking his lips.

Later on, wiping grease from his chin, Okot said, "That's the best thing I ever ate. Ever."

"Me too," Paul said with a sigh. "Better than Christmas."

Christmas, Okot thought. That's something that Christians have. Mandy and Elisha had tried to explain to Okot about Christmas. It had to do with their Jesus God. Okot said, "Paul, d'you know about a black book called a Bible?"

Paul's eyes widened. "Well, sure. Of course I do. My father is a preacher. A—man of God. He tells people about the Bible."

"Then you know!" Okot exclaimed. "You wrote in the Bible. You said there's no slaves nor free men."

Paul was puzzled. And Okot was scared. Should he tell Paul that he was a runaway slave? No. Not yet. He said, "Someone called Paul wrote in that black book."

"Oh." Now Paul understood. "You mean the *apostle* Paul. He was a man who loved God. He lived hundreds and hundreds of years ago. He wrote parts of the Bible. Not me. My father called me Paul because he wanted me to grow up to be a man of God too. Like Paul of the Bible."

Okot slumped in disappointment, kicking a clod of dirt into the fire.

"Why d'you want to know about slaves and free men?" Paul asked.

Okot said, "You come from the country of slave traders!"

Paul was startled. "Everyone's not a slave trader in England. Lots of men think it's wrong."

Okot thought about this in silence.

It was very late now. Outside, they heard an owl hooting. Chip said to Paul, "You sleep here?"

"Can I stay with you?"

Okot and Chip glanced at each other. In a moment they nodded yes. Paul smiled. "Thanks," he said, and brought in his bedroll and oilskin. He was shivering from the cold and damp. He spread the oilskin on the ground, and then the thick bedroll, beside the bed of evergreen branches.

The fire and good food had left them all warm and drowsy. Chip thought, *We shouldn't leave the goose here. An animal might smell it....* But he was too comfortable to be bothered getting up. He didn't even think that it was the first time in his life—except when he was mauled by the bear and couldn't do anything—that he didn't obey all that he had been taught about the ways of the forest.

In spite of their tiredness they were a long time going to sleep. They couldn't move without bumping against each other. Chip lay down with one arm on his bow. Okot kept hold of the knife at his waist, and wondered about English slave traders and English men of God.

Paul had never slept near an Indian before. And he didn't know what to make of Okot. But finally he thought, *My father came here to bring the gospel to Chip's people. Maybe God brought me to him, and to Okot, too.* And he fell into an uneasy sleep.

A strange scrabbling noise jerked Okot awake. He stared into the darkness, straining to see. The fire had gone out. There it was again—the scraping of claws against the rocky overhang of their shelter. What was it? *"Chip!"* he whispered fiercely.

But Chip was already awake. As his eyes adjusted to the dark, Okot saw Chip draw his knife from its sheath. There was more scratching outside. Loose stones fell across the entrance. Suddenly Okot found himself facing two glaring eyes and a ferocious snout. He couldn't see the body of the creature at all. It snapped up the remains of the goose that they had left by the fire, crushing the bones in one bite of its powerful jaws. Okot thought, *We must all smell like goose. What if it comes after us?*

"Stay back," Chip hissed. "It want meat."

"Wolverine!" Paul whispered. He picked up a stick and threw it at the beast. The wolverine snarled and snapped. And then it attacked! It seemed to fly at Paul, a black shadow in the night. The long curved claws raked at the white boy. Okot shrank back as Chip flung his knife at it. And then Paul was stabbing at it with his own knife. It snapped and writhed and kept coming at Paul. There was the sticky black smell all around them of blood and wet fur, and then they were all lunging at the creature and yelling at the top of their lungs.

Finally, after what seemed like hours, silence fell. Outside, dawn was breaking. The boys looked at each other, and then around the shelter. The wolverine was gone, but there was a dark smeary trail across the flattened grass and out toward the woods. Paul was sitting with his back against the rock, holding onto his shoulder and saying, "Ow, ow, ow," softly to himself, over and over again.

"Paul," Okot said, crawling over to him. "You hurt bad?"

"No, not bad," he said, but his voice was thin and shaky.

"Is very bad beast," Chip said. "Is most hurting. But make good fur for cold moon times."

"Yeah," Paul said. "I wish I'd made that one into a fur hat."

After a while, when they were breathing easier and the sky was pink with the morning sun, the three of them went down to the stream to wash. They waded into the current in their clothes to clean off the blood, and the water swirled red all around them. "Good thing there's no crocodiles in this river," Okot said. Paul understood him and grinned, even though his face was pale and sick-looking. He pulled off his ripped shirt and washed the gouges in his shoulder. They were long and ugly, but not too deep.

"Now we be like two braves," Chip said, showing Paul his injured leg.

Paul was impressed. "Was it a bear? Like your horse?"

So Chip, with Okot's help, told the story of his adventures, while they sat on the bank of the stream and waited for the sun to dry them off.

They groaned when they went back to the shelter. It smelled terrible, like something rotting. There was blood all over their bed of evergreens, and on Paul's bedroll, and the ashes from the fire had been scattered everywhere. They followed the wolverine's trail until it disappeared into the woods, and Chip said, "It go die. Not live more. Not come back."

"I hope you's right," Okot said fervently.

"It my wrong," Chip said miserably. "Not good leave food here. Make these bad animal come."

"I guess we all know better," Paul said. "I was too tired to think about it."

"Onondaga brave must know better," Chip said.

"Fine, then," Okot said, grinning. "We gonna make Onondaga brave pay for his mistake. Come'n help us clean up this mess."

It took them most of the morning. They hauled out all the evergreen branches and burned them by the side of the stream. They soaked the blood off Paul's bedroll and laid it out in the sun to dry. Then they carried water from the stream, in Paul's tin pot and enamel mug, and Chip's birch-bark bowl, to wash down the grass. Afterwards, they cut fresh spruce branches and made a new bed, along the back wall of the shelter, thick and deep, big enough for the three of them.

All the time that they were working, Okot and Chip kept sneaking glances at Paul. *He's so different from Payne and Master Abbot,* Okot thought. *He's nice—even nicer than Mrs. Abbot. And he knows this Jesus God Savior, just like Mandy and Elisha.* He shook his head and carried on sweeping up the scattered coals from the fire pit. Paul and Chip were spreading Paul's oilskin over the fresh evergreen bed. Okot's thoughts buzzed around in his head like a swarm of bees. *All of the people like Chip have their Great Spirit god, but they still have wars against each other. But Paul doesn't seem to have any hate in him. I wonder if he's different from other white men. I wonder if we can trust him.*

Chip was confused. Paul seemed so different from the white men that his father and grandfather talked about. He hadn't complained at all about his shoulder, even though Chip knew it must be hurting him. Paul had gone with Chip to look at Proudfoot's wounds, and then he took a turn standing with the horse in the stream. *He smiles a lot,* Chip thought. *Even though he must be scared. I wonder what happened to his father? White men don't know the ways of the forest, but Paul's lived all this time by himself, since he lost his father.* For the first time in his life, Chip found himself thinking, *Maybe Thunder Arm is wrong. Maybe there are some white men we can trust.*

Chapter 13

Trappers and Other Troubles

By the time the sun was high in the sky they were ravenous. Chip shot two trout, and he and Paul cleaned them while Okot filled the birch-bark bowl with berries. All the time, he watched Chip and Paul. He noticed that Chip kept his bow near him, with an arrow ready on the string.

Paul watched Chip out of the corner of his eye. *Is Chip from the same tribe of Indians that attacked us?* he wondered. *Is he Iroquois? Should I ask him about it? Would he know what happened to my father?* He finished gutting the fish and cleaned his knife. He noticed that Chip watched carefully every movement he made. *He doesn't trust me,* he thought. *But I guess I don't blame him. I'm not sure how far I can trust him either.*

These thoughts kept them quiet while they cooked and ate the fish by the stream. But finally Paul broke the silence. "Chip, are your people at war right now?"

Chip scowled. "Onondaga only make big hunt. For bear and deer."

"So what does it mean when they paint their faces?"

"Why ask this? You saw painted Onondaga?"

"I don't know what tribe they were from. But that's how I lost my father. We were attacked by a war party.

Braves on horses." He swallowed hard. "Do you think they would kill him?"

Chip frowned. "I not hear about this. Is maybe other tribe. Not from my village. Not from Ohsweken."

"But would they scalp him?" Paul persisted.

"I tell you, I not know!" Chip shouted. "White men do bad things. Braves hate white men."

Paul was silent. *Dear Jesus,* he thought, *help me to trust you the way I should. And help me to make friends with Chip and Okot.*

Okot had listened to Chip and Paul talking. *Can we ever be friends?* he wondered. He wanted to talk to Paul more about his Jesus God, but Chip's face was black as thunder and he didn't want to upset him any more.

Suddenly Paul said, "How did you get here, Okot? Where are you from?"

Okot's heart thumped in his chest. *Should I tell him? Elisha said I would be safe here, so it can't hurt. Maybe he can help me to find a place to live, and work, when we get back to his white man's village.* His stomach churned and he felt sick, the way he had when Payne whipped him with the hickory stick. But finally, he said, "I was a slave. On a plantation in a place called Virginia. I runned away, 'cause Payne—the overseer—him was a terrible bad man. Hateful. He was always beatin' us slaves. An' I didn't like belongin' to men, like I was just a dog. Them other slaves, they's said if I could get to Upper Canada, then I could live like a free man. Jus' like white men."

Paul nodded. "My father told me that there's lots of escaped slaves coming to Upper Canada. Specially down further south from here, in a place called Amherstburg."

"Maybe that's where I should go, then," Okot said thoughtfully.

"My father can help you get there, once we get back to Brant's Ford, and find him," Paul said. *If he's still alive,* he added to himself. *But I have to believe he is.*

"So, when Chip's leg is better, and Proudfoot too, we gonna go together?" Okot asked.

Chip and Paul looked at each other. Then Chip looked at the ground. His thoughts were like a whirling blizzard inside him. Finally, he said, "I think on this. Is hard thing, for Onondaga to travel with white man. Great Spirit be angry." Then he looked up. A tiny smile broke through his frown. "But you not like all white men. You got brave heart."

Paul laughed in relief. He thought it was almost worth getting clawed by the wolverine, to hear Chip say that he was like a brave.

Later that day, while Chip held Proudfoot in the stream for his "water medicine," Okot and Paul went off into the forest with one of Paul's saddlebags to look for nuts and berries. It was chilly in the shadow of the thick trees and they quickened their steps to keep warm.

"Fall's coming soon," Paul said, rubbing his hands together. "All the Indians say that it's going to be a long winter."

Okot nodded. He was concentrating on signs of a fresh trail. Suddenly he stopped dead, putting a finger to his lips. He pointed out, to Paul, an "X" that had recently been carved on the trunk of a cedar tree. Paul's eyes widened. Silently, they crept forward, and found another "X" on a tree a few yards ahead.

"A trapper," Paul whispered in Okot's ear. "Marking out his trails—where he's going to lay his traps in the winter."

They went on, treading quietly. They saw more signs of the trapper—broken branches and freshly scuffed soil. In another ten or fifteen minutes they came to a camp. There was a blackened circle where someone had made a fire, and a tin cooking pot and a kettle hung from a low tree branch. A bedroll lay in the shelter of a spreading spruce, and next to it a stained old oilskin was stretched over a bundle of furs.

Paul pointed to them. "Beaver pelts," he whispered. "Trappers often bring them to the trading posts, to exchange for things like salt and flour."

"What's a beaver?" Okot asked.

There didn't seem to be anyone around. Paul slipped over to the pelts and pulled one out. "This," he said. "They live in rivers and streams. These pelts make great hats. Nice and warm and they keep the rain and snow out. The trappers and Indians eat the meat too."

Okot stroked the dark-brown fur. It was like nothing he had ever felt before, smooth and thick and slightly oily. "How'd they catch'em?" he asked.

"With traps," Paul said. They had forgotten to be so careful, and he was wandering around the little camp. Behind the pile of pelts, a heap of traps was stashed under another oilskin. He held one up to show Okot. Just then, they both heard someone coming toward them through the trees, whistling a tune. Paul dropped the trap. Okot dropped the beaver pelt, and they ran back toward their clearing.

"We should've put them things back," Okot said, when they were well away from the camp. "What if'n he thinks we was tryin' to rob'im?"

"A trapper wouldn't hurt us," Paul said. But he didn't sound very sure of himself.

"D'you think he's got a gun?"

"Sure," Paul said, slowing to a walk. "They all do. But they're not crazy. And we didn't take anything."

They were both breathing hard when they came to the edge of their clearing. In spite of Paul's reassurances they kept looking back over their shoulders.

"Is bear chasing you?" Chip asked when he saw them. He was sitting at the entrance to their shelter, carving feather sticks with his knife.

Paul flung himself down on the grass. "No. But we found a trapper's camp. Not very far from here."

"Was raccoons in any trap? Something good for meat?"

"I don't know," Paul said, frowning. "But we couldn't take anything anyway. That would be stealing."

"Not stealing," Chip objected. "Is many raccoons in this woods."

"Good," Okot interrupted. "Then why don't our Onondaga brave shoot one for supper?"

"Oh, no!" Paul said suddenly. "My saddlebag!"

"What?" Okot said.

"I—I put it down, when we looked at the beaver pelts. I forgot to pick it up again."

They stared, horrified at each other.

"It's okay," Okot said after a while. "We didn't take nothin'. An' we can do without it. Right, Paul?"

He grinned weakly. "I guess we have to."

But none of them slept well that night.

The next morning Chip was gone when Okot and Paul got up. They crawled out of the shelter, and in the misty gray light stumbled over a furry animal lying on the grass. "Ugh!" Paul grunted. "Chip, where are you?"

"Aiee!" Chip yelled, and slid down on top of them from the rocky overhang. "Onondaga brave make good hunting while black and white men sleep."

"You got a raccoon!" Paul said, turning the dead creature over with his foot. "But we wanted it for supper, not breakfast."

"When we make roast, it smell so good you want for breakfast," Chip assured him. "Who make fire? Who clean raccoon?"

"I'll get wood," Okot said. He left Paul and Chip and went off into the trees. It was a damp morning, and it took him quite a while to find enough dry twigs and branches. He wandered happily, picking up bits of wood and cones from the forest floor. He sang softly the song Mandy had taught him. "Swing low, sweet chariot, comin' for to carry me home."

The sudden cracking of a twig made him whirl around. He was face to face with a white man—and a white man's gun.

The man shouted at him, but Okot didn't understand the language. He was dressed in a buckskin shirt and leggings, and wearing a red woolen cap. His face was unshaven and his voice was hoarse and rough. Around his waist was a wide buckskin sash, and in it was stuck a knife and a small axe. He shouted again at Okot, and pushed the barrel of the gun into his bony chest.

Chip and Paul were sitting by the fire in their shelter, breathing in the good fat smell of the roasting raccoon and talking about Chip's family in Ohsweken, when Okot reappeared. "Too late," Paul laughed. "We had to build a fire on our own. We thought you left already for Amherstburg."

Okot shook his head dumbly, and glanced back over his shoulder. Paul and Chip looked behind him. Paul's face went very white. Chip's was like stone. The trapper waved his gun, and shoved Okot down. He spoke again, his words hard and angry.

"He's French," Paul said. "I think he's saying we stole things. His beaver pelts and traps. And now this raccoon…" His voice trailed off as the trapper pressed the barrel of his gun against Paul's chest. "Dear God, please help us," Paul whispered. He didn't even realize he had prayed out loud.

"D'you really think your Jesus God can help us now?" Okot said.

"Of course," Paul whispered back. He spoke to the trapper, slowly, because he had to think of the French words. "*Nous ne sommes pas voleurs. C'est mon ami qui a tué le—le—*" He stopped, and then pointed to the roasting raccoon. He didn't know what it was called in French.

The trapper grunted, and turned his gun on Chip. The Indian boy started talking to him in his own language. To their utter astonishment, the trapper responded, waving his arms, pointing back through the woods, and shouting louder and louder. Okot shivered with fright. He thought that the gun might go off and kill one of them.

Finally the trapper stopped talking. Chip turned to his friends. "Him say someone stealed all his beavers. Stealed all animals from his traps. Him not got food, not got pelts for trading." He added unnecessarily, "Him very mad with us."

For the moment Okot's curiosity made him forget their danger. "How come he knows your language, Chip?"

"Chipagawana!" Chip said, which he only did now when he was really tense or bad-tempered. Then he shrugged. "All this French trappers, them know how speak to us. How else we make trades with them? I tell him we not take him pelts. I tell him look here. Look at all we got." He turned back to the trapper and spoke again in Onondaga, pointing to the roasting meat. "I tell him I shoot raccoon with my bow and arrow. I tell him he can eat with us."

The trapper pushed past the three of them and looked into the shelter. He picked up the bedroll and shook it, and searched among the evergreen branches. Then he grunted again, and, still waving his gun threateningly, he walked around the clearing. He poked in all the clumps of bushes. He overturned Paul's saddle. The boys sat without moving. They hardly dared to breathe. But at last the trapper returned. He looked less grim, but now he was shaking his head sadly. He and Chip talked some more, and then he wheeled around and stalked off into the trees.

"Him say okay, we maybe not steal. Him say he look some more, find what man took his things."

When the raccoon was ready they ate in silence. Normally they would have enjoyed the rich and delicious meat. They would have laughed at each other, with the grease running down their chins and wrists, and looked forward to washing off afterwards as they swam in the stream. But after their encounter with the trapper none of them had any appetite.

They had eaten their fill, and were straightening out the mess the trapper had made of their bed, when he reappeared out of the woods. "Oh, no," Okot groaned, but then he and Paul cried, "Yippee!" together. This time the trapper's gun was safely slung harmlessly over his shoulder, and he was carrying Paul's saddlebag. He dropped it on the ground, and said something to Chip.

"Him say sorry for scaring us," Chip explained. "And can he have something to eat?"

"*Oui, oui, oui!*" Paul said, the one French word he was really sure of. "Yes, of course he can." He cut off a great hunk of meat and offered it to the trapper. The man ate standing up. Chip peppered him with questions, and Paul and Okot heard the words "Ohsweken" and "Onondaga" several times. The trapper answered between bites, and then he left with a backwards wave of his hand.

"Him say we be more than eight days' riding from my village of Ohsweken," Chip told them. "Him say we must go north until we come to hill country. Maybe six or seven days' riding. This Onondaga country. Then we must go east, to rising sun. This come to Ohsweken. We must be quiet. Not make big fires. Him say is many war parties. Is trouble coming to place we call Thundering Waters. Niagara. We must go careful. Him say also we must watch horses. Man who stole his beaver pelts and traps maybe steal our horses. Him say we keep horses close to shelter in the nights. And we must go soon. Already wolves and fox and other animals begin make fur for cold moons. Soon snow come."

Finally, Chip ran out of words and breath. It was the longest speech he had ever made. Paul said, "I don't think he was so terrible after all. I think he's just sad over losing his things. It would be nice if he came with us."

Chip shook his head. "Him losted all summer's work. Now, him go other way, to lake called Erie. Try to find some work, make white man's money to buy more traps."

Paul looked across the clearing to where the horses were grazing. He frowned. "It would be awful if someone stole Storm or Proudfoot. It would take us weeks and weeks to walk back to—" He stopped. "Back to where?" he said, almost to himself. "I have to go back to Brant's Ford. Or maybe Middleport."

"Ohsweken not long from Brant's Ford," Chip said.

"But you don't know what your father will do with Okot and me," Paul insisted. "How can we stay together?"

They looked at each other, and saw doubt and a little fear in each other's eyes. Then Okot said firmly, "We's got many days of ridin' before we's got to decide what to do. An' many days before we can get goin' anyways. Chip an' Proudfoot gotta get real better."

They nodded, glad to put off having to think any more about the future. That evening, they led the horses close to their shelter. Chip and Paul carved the ends of two sturdy branches to sharp points, and then Okot helped Paul pound them into the ground with a flat rock. They tied each horse to a stake with the reins from Storm's bridle and Proudfoot's hackamore, so that they couldn't move out of their sight.

At first Okot objected. "This'll make 'em easier to steal," he said.

But Paul and Chip disagreed. "Proudfoot make big crying and kicking if anyone try," Chip said. "This way we hear for sure."

They were tired out from the adventures of the day, but it was hard to sleep because they were so worried about the thief who might be nearby. Paul, as usual, took out his Bible and read for a few minutes by firelight. Chip made feather sticks, and Okot watched Paul curiously. He saw him turn away to face the darkness, and knew he was praying to his Jesus God. Okot was bursting to ask Paul more questions about his God.

They must finally have gone to sleep, because they were jolted awake by a loud crash of thunder. Lightning flashed around them. Rain poured down and lashed into the shelter. Then there was a booming crack of thunder right over their heads and the whole clearing lit up bright as day.

Okot huddled against the back of the shelter, his eyes wide. Were the tribal spirits fighting again with the Great Spirit? Okot's skin was clammy, his mouth dry with fear.

Paul stuck his head out and looked around. Storm and Proudfoot were prancing restlessly, whinnying and pulling against their stakes. Lightning slashed down again, striking a tall spruce tree at the edge of the forest behind them. "Look out!" Paul shouted. He dashed outside and tried to untie Storm. In his hurry he fumbled at the knots and the wet leather slipped in his hands. The horses were pulling frantically now, sensing danger. In despair, Paul hauled at one of the stakes. Out of the corner of his eye he saw Okot yanking at the other one. There was a ferocious crack and a great swoosh in the air above them. The horses panicked and reared back. The loosened stakes came out of the ground with sluggish gurgles, and the terrified creatures bolted.

The spruce tree had been split right down the middle and was burning. Paul and Okot saw half of the trunk swaying, and then it began falling toward them. They ducked back inside, where Chip was working feverishly to keep burning wood and coals from being blown onto their evergreen bed.

A second later the tree crashed down onto their shelter. The three boys cringed back against the rock wall. Small branches broke and scattered, smacking them like whips. A large branch broke off and whammed into the fire, scattering burning wood and coals again. Okot yelped and jumped sideways as hot ashes spattered on his bare foot. He landed on top of Chip, who toppled over onto Paul.

When they realized they were still safe, they grinned nervously at each other. They sorted themselves out and inspected the damage. Chip took up one of their evergreen boughs and used it to sweep the coals back onto the stone fire pit. They piled twigs and broken branches on the fire and soon it was blazing warmly against the darkness and the storm.

Chip suddenly laughed. "Great Spirit send more wood for our fire!"

Paul and Okot laughed with him as they inspected the jam of branches now wedged solidly over the opening to their shelter. "Now we have a real house," Paul said. "Walls all around."

Okot stuck his burned foot out in the rain for a few minutes, until it stopped smarting. Then he sat down again with the others, with his back against the rock wall. Their faces were wet with rainwater and sweat. Outside, the rain thrummed down heavily, but there was no wind now. The fire soon dried them out.

Once the lightning faded away, and thunder only rumbled in the distance like the growling of a lion, Okot and Paul went out to retrieve the horses. This time they tied them to the sturdy branches of the fallen tree. After they had dried off again they lay down gratefully with Chip. This time, they had no trouble falling asleep.

Chapter 14

The Slave Raiders

Okot dreamed he was back in Africa, watching in the distance the great herds of zebra and wildebeest that roamed the grasslands under the hot yellow sun. He smiled in his sleep. Now he dreamed that he was in the fields with his father's cattle and goats. He could hear his father calling him. "Okot Deng, keep your eyes sharp! Some of the men have seen a lion nearby."

In his dream, Okot ran with a sharp stick in his hand to make the goats come back to the main flock. *Boom!* He heard the crack of a gun.

Okot sat up so fast that his head swam. He was breathing hard, and his face was wet with sweat. For a minute he couldn't remember where he was.

Slowly he realized it was just a dream. His eyes adjusted to the dimness and he could see Chip and Paul sleeping. He felt the soft bed of evergreens under him. The rain was still coming down, hard and heavy like a waterfall. Thunder rumbled all around the clearing. Okot took a deep breath and peered out of their shelter. *It must be morning,* he thought, but the sky was blue-black with storm clouds.

Paul stirred and sat up. "What's wrong?" he asked sleepily. "Not the thief, I hope."

Instantly, Chip was awake, reaching for his bow and quiver of arrows. "Is white man there?" he whispered.

The other two laughed. "Only Paul," Okot said. "I had a bad dream. But it was a true dream. About Africa, when the slave raiders came."

"You should tell us about it," Paul said. His stomach grumbled, and they laughed. "I mean, after breakfast."

Chip and Paul broke a few branches off the fallen tree, making an easier way out of the shelter. Okot rescued the rest of their roasted raccoon meat, which they had stored overnight in one of the saddlebags hanging from a tree by the stream—safely away from the shelter. They finished it up, washing it down with more of Chip's birch-bark tea. Afterwards they sat at the edge of their shelter, looking out at the storm, and Okot told them his story.

The black boy closed his eyes and thought of the wide plains beside the river Lol, the tall grasses that waved in the wind where he had played with his friends, and his dog Diling. He sighed, and looked at his two new friends. "I had many sisters and brothers," he said, "and many friends. Maybe some's still alive in Nyamlel." He pointed to Chip. "You're Onondaga. I am Monyjang. What others—*juur*—call Dinka tribe." Chip nodded, understanding. "My father—" Okot stopped. His throat felt funny, and his stomach hurt. He could almost hear his father's voice. "At nighttime," he said, "my father and th'other men sat by the fires an' talked about our great country—about the Monyjang and all that we got because we make offerings against sickness and death."

"Like Onondaga," Chip said. "Every night, in longhouse, braves speak great wars of our fathers."

Okot frowned. "Monyjang ain't like braves," he said. "We likes peace. We's always havin' great feasts, an' many men come from over the grass and water from other tribes to eat at our tables." He swallowed hard. "But then the slave raiders come. There was loud boomin' noises from all over, and from the village, an' people was cryin' and screamin'. My father run back to our village. He had his spear in his hand. We didn't know what was all the bangin' noises."

"Guns," Paul said.

"Yeah. Big guns. I tries to hide, up in a tamarind tree. But they finds me. They's tied my hands an' took me to the village. They's already tied up many men, an' the strong women. My mother was tied up with'em. And another one of my father's wives—"

"Your father had more than one wife?" Paul interrupted, astonished.

Okot stared at him blankly. "Sure. I think he must'a had six or seven wives. Our village weren't too big. Some of them chiefs what came, they had lots more."

Paul chewed this over in silence. He wondered why his father had never told him about things like that.

"So they's pointed guns at us," Okot went on. "A friend o'mine tried to run away, but one of them raiders pointed his gun at him an' boom! An' he's fell down dead."

Paul said, "I had a friend who was killed too. During an Indian raid." He had only meant to tell Okot that he knew how he felt. But when he saw Chip's angry face he was sorry he'd said anything.

"Many Onondaga die too," Chip said.

"Next thing," Okot said quickly, "I tries to see my father." He rubbed his eyes with the backs of his hands. "He weren't with us. I saw him later, when the raiders took us out from the village. He was lyin' on the ground, with blood comin' out of his stomach. Dinka spears weren't no good to fight them guns."

"Who were they?" Paul asked. "The people who tied you up? Were they like me? English?"

Okot shook his head. "Some was black, like us Monyjang. Dinka. But these was short. They talked a strange language. Some of 'em had pale faces, like this." Okot showed them the palms of his hands. "Later, I heard them's called Arabs. But some of 'em was from our own tribe. They's sold us, like we was enemies. I don't know this word in English."

"Traitor," Paul said. His face was very pale.

"Traitor." Okot tried the word on his tongue. "Terrible bad men. Traitors." Okot remembered that bright hot day, and how cold he had felt because he was so scared. "They's put chains on us," he said. He showed Paul and Chip the scars around his neck and ankles. "An' they made us walk. All of 'em had whips. They tooked our goats too, an' made them women carry sacks of millet, an' dried cassava root."

"What happened to everyone else in the village?" Paul asked.

Okot shrugged. "I never saw 'em. Them raiders must've left the old people. An' the weaker women. I had lots of sisters. And brothers. Maybe some was caught too. I dunno, 'cause they took so many different lots of people. Some babies cried. We could hear 'em. But then we was too far away. They made us walk to the sunset. West."

"Was long walk?" Chip wanted to know.

"Very long. We walked for three moons." Okot shuddered. "An' we's always hungry. They beat us to make us walk. Time were someone fell, an' we all got beat with whips. Lots died. We got fevers, and was starvin' an' had sores all over. They jus' took off the chains from the dead people an' left'em there in the forest. They's called'em 'hyena bait.' But there was always more people, from other tribes, an' they got chained up with us."

For a while, Okot stopped talking. The rain drummed on the roof of their shelter. The fire had burned down to embers. Paul went out, and came back in a few minutes with an armful of dry branches and pinecones from the forest.

Chip said to Okot, "Soon this white man be wise brave like us."

Paul laughed. He smacked himself on his chest with his fist. "Wise white man know fire," he said. "Wise white man like things cozy." He stirred up the fire and added some of the wood. Steam rose off his wet shirt.

"What mean 'cozy'?" Chip asked.

"Cups of tea?" Paul said, and he and Okot snorted with laughter. Okot thought of Mrs. Abbot and her lady friends. They used to drink tea in their long rustling skirts on the veranda of the plantation house. *This is much more cozy,* he thought, looking around their shelter.

Chip frowned. He hated it when Paul and Okot said things he couldn't understand. So Paul tried to explain "cozy" to him. "Like in your longhouse," he said. "When you have a fire burning, and good food, and warm furs and everything is safe. That's cozy."

But Okot was thinking about the rain that had poured down on him and the other captives in the forests of Africa. He remembered how the heavy chains bit into his skin. Suddenly, forgetting where he was, he jumped up, and banged his head on the rock ledge. "Ow ow!" he shouted, rubbing the bump. But then he remembered something else. "We couldn't never talk," he said. "Or them raiders beat us. They beat the women when they cried. They beat my mother." He leaped out of the shelter into the pouring rain, waving his arms above his head. "Aiee!" he cried, imitating Chip. "No one *never* gonna beat me again! No one *never* gonna chain me up again!"

Chip and Paul jumped out into the rain with Okot, laughing with relief because their friend had looked so sad and angry when he was telling them his story. Now he was grinning as he ran around the clearing. He pulled off his soaking shirt and waved it over his head. "I am Monyjang!" he yelled. "Not a slave!" He threw his shirt on the grass and ran toward the woods, pretending he was hunting with a spear. Then he climbed a tree, and hung from the branches with his long thin legs and arms dangling like the black snakes of Africa. This time he pretended he had a gun and was shooting at the slave raiders.

Paul and Chip joined in, throwing their shirts on the ground and punching at each other. "Take that, and that!" Paul shouted, jabbing the air in front of Chip. Then Okot said "Boom!" from the tree. Paul grabbed at his chest, as though he had really been shot, and fell to the ground.

"Slave raider dead!" Chip cried. "Aiee!" And Okot jumped down from his tree laughing.

Paul stood up, wiping the wet grass from his face. Chip and Okot looked at each other. "Him not dead yet!" Chip said, and they both jumped on Paul. All three of them fell to the ground, wrestling like tigers.

Soon Chip had to give up and roll away. His leg was cramped and throbbing with pain again. But Okot and Paul tumbled about furiously. Okot was taller than Paul, lean and agile. Paul was heavier, and his shoulders were wide and strong. They were a good match for each other. He and Okot had their legs locked together. They panted as they slithered around on the muddy ground, trying to get a grip on each other.

Suddenly, a huge crack of thunder split the air. The rain came down so hard that they could hardly see a thing. They flung themselves apart, laughing and breathing hard. Chip said, "You be like bear cubs."

Okot got up on his knees and made a growling noise, deep in his throat. It sounded so real that Paul jerked his head around, trying to see into the forest. "It's only me," Okot said, grinning. "Black Africa bear."

The rain pelted down on them. Okot turned his face up to the sky with his mouth wide open. Paul noticed how perfect and white his teeth were against his black skin. Then he remembered what his father had once told him. "Some of the tribes in Africa are cannibals. They eat people from other tribes."

Paul had been horrified. He wondered if Okot belonged to one of those tribes. The idea fascinated and scared him at the same time.

Chip interrupted his thoughts. "Is fish belly I see?" he said suddenly, pointing at Paul's bare white skin. "No! Is white man's belly!" He looked at Paul's face and his eyes were twinkling. Okot stood next to Paul, and the contrast between them made them all shriek with laughter.

"Now see brown Onondaga fish!" Chip shouted. He pulled off his soaking clothes and dived into the middle of the stream. It was swollen with the rain and the water overflowed the banks.

Paul laughed when Chip's brown body appeared again above the rushing water. "Okot!" he called, so Chip could hear him. "Get the bow and arrow! I see our lunch." Then they both stripped off their muddy grass-stained pants and jumped in with Chip. They splashed and chased each other with pretend spears.

"Arrrgh!" Chip shouted suddenly.

Okot turned and saw Chip's head disappearing under the water. "Paul!" he cried. "Chip needs help!"

Paul was closest. He dived after Chip and pulled him up quickly, out of the swirling current. They sat on the flooded grass beside the stream, panting.

"Is leg," Chip gasped. His face was twisted with pain. "I think is bad spirit in leg. Spirit from bear come in me when bear claws open me up." He rubbed his shaking leg hard with his hands. "Is no good for brave," he said.

Okot swam over and hauled himself out of the water. "What happened?"

"I think he has a bad cramp," Paul said.

"Is bear spirit," Chip insisted. "It war with spirit of my Hotahyonhne clan. Thunder Arm be shamed by me," Chip said miserably. "No good brave."

Paul squirmed uncomfortably at Chip's talk about animal spirits. He knew it was part of the Iroquois religion, but he wanted to tell Chip that it wasn't true—that there was only one true Spirit, the God who would never hurt him. But he knew Chip wasn't ready to hear it from him right then. So he said instead, "Thunder Arm will be proud of you. How many Onondaga braves do you know who've been attacked by a bear?"

"Is many hunt bear."

"Is different thing," Paul said. He imitated Chip's voice so perfectly that Chip and Okot both laughed.

"I'm hungry," Okot said. "What'll we eat for lunch? I guess there won't be no trout today."

"We find rabbit maybe," Chip said. "In trees where is not raining."

Paul and Okot helped him limp across the clearing to the woods, and Okot fetched the bow and quiver of arrows from the shelter. Chip sat quietly, patiently, in the shelter of a spruce tree, with an arrow ready on the string. Paul went off to find dry wood and pinecones for the fire. Okot sat with Chip, worried that Chip's leg might cramp up on him again and that he would have trouble getting up. All around them rain dripped off the tree branches and made little plopping sounds when it hit the forest floor.

They seemed to wait for hours before Okot saw Chip's hand tighten on his bow. *He's seen something,* he thought. *Or heard something. I hope it's good to eat.*

There was a faint clicking sound from up in the branches of a maple tree, and the scraping of claws on wood. Okot thought he recognized the noises, but it was not something he had heard in the New World. It reminded him of the porcupines that rattled their quills from the trees in Africa whenever anyone went by.

Twang! Chip's arrow zinged through the air. There was a muffled whump and the porcupine tumbled to the ground. It was smaller than those Okot remembered, and the spiny quills were much shorter. The porcupines in Nyamlel had quills as long as his forearm.

He helped Chip to his feet and they retrieved the dead porcupine. "Is very good food," Chip said with satisfaction. He held it in place with the arrow, and slit it quickly along the belly. In no time at all he had gutted it, and he carried his prize back to the clearing with Okot supporting him. They washed the meat in the stream, and then Paul spitted it and set it to roasting over the fire he had made.

Paul had always found porcupine a strange-tasting meat when he'd eaten it at the homes of settlers he visited with his father. In fact, he'd never wanted to eat it again. But living in the bush had changed his tastes. He was as ravenous as Chip and Okot, and could hardly wait while the plump meat roasted. There was a lot of fat on it that sizzled and spattered as it dripped onto the fire, and the mouth-watering smell made their stomachs hurt with hunger. When Chip finally poked the meat and said it was ready, they ate as though they hadn't had food in a week.

Okot was sitting, as usual, with his legs out in front of him. Paul watched him chewing the porcupine meat, and he thought again about Okot's tribe and cannibals. He was dying to ask the question, but he didn't know how. Finally he just blurted out, "Okot, do you Dinka eat people?"

Okot stopped chewing. Nothing showed on his face—not surprise or anger. He looked completely serious when he said, "Not less'n we roast'em first." Then he burst out laughing at the expression on Paul's face.

Paul's face went beet red. "My father once told me that some tribes in Africa eat people," Paul said. "I—I'm sorry. I shouldn't have asked."

Okot grinned. "My tribe don't. But my father..." His voice caught in his throat. "My father told me about a man he met from the Congo. The man pinched my father's cheek an' said, 'That's the best tastin' part.' My father give him a little poke with his spear, an' tol' him to go away."

Paul shuddered. Then he and Okot both looked at Chip.

Chip hesitated. Finally he said, "Onondaga not eat people. But is true. Some Haudenosaunee tribes do." He hung his head. "You still want be my friends?"

Their eyes flicked from one to another. Then Okot giggled nervously. "So long as you promise you only roast coons an' porcupines an' trout!"

"Aiee!" Chip cried, and gave his warrior yips. "Okay. White and black men I eat raw!" He picked up another hunk of porcupine and took a huge bite, baring his teeth like a wolf. They all snorted with laughter, and felt better, because they had finally talked about what had been on their minds ever since they met.

Outside the shelter the sky was dark with boiling, angry clouds. The rain kept coming down. When they had finished and washed their greasy hands and chins with rainwater, they curled up under Paul's warm bedroll, and Okot told them more about the slave raiders.

"We come to a place where the land stopped, an' there was nothin' but water." Okot spread his arms wide. "Not a river. There was nuthin' on th'other side. The water went right out to the sky." He tried to describe the beach to Chip and Okot. "There was a wide place, where nothin' grew. The trees stopped, an' there was white stuff on the ground, very soft, an' it burned our feet."

"That's sand, on a beach," Paul said. "My father told me about the slave trade. They make all their captives walk to the edge of the Atlantic Ocean. That's the same water I sailed across from England."

"Yes, ocean," Okot said. "I learned that word later, on the ship. We didn' know what was salty water, when we got there. They pushed us down to the water an' made us wash. We tried to drink it, we's so thirsty. We was all sick. An' when it dried, it made my skin itch all over."

"They kept us in a place on the beach, with walls made of thorn bushes. There was more people brought every day, from different tribes. An' one white man in charge. He's called Factor. Every day he shouted at us, I think in English, but we didn't know none then. They gave us bread an' water." Okot picked up a bone and gnawed at it with satisfaction. He would never forget what it was like to be hungry all the time.

"We was all scared about what was gonna happen. There was a huge ship floatin' on the water. We could see it, but it never went nowhere. Then, one day, some white men came an' looked at us. They shouted at each other an' looked in our mouths an' felt our arms and legs." Okot made a face. "Jus' like my father looked to see if a cow was strong."

Okot shuddered suddenly. Chip and Paul looked at each other across the fire, wondering what was coming next. Okot pushed away the bedroll and pointed to a strange scar on his chest. The skin was puckered, like an old burn. "They took us all out from the prison, a few at a time. There was a big fire they kept burnin' on the beach, all day and night. They's held me an' burned me here. With the iron made hot from the fire."

Paul gasped. "A branding iron!" he said. He had helped homesteaders many times, branding cattle and horses. He remembered the squeals of the animals and the stink of burning hair and flesh. He liked branding time. It was exciting to wrestle with the calves and foals, getting dusty and gritty just like the other men. Besides, it had to be done, and didn't hurt the animals for very long. But that was different from doing it to a person.

For the second time in his life, just like after he heard about his friend Freeman being scalped, Paul felt something ugly churning inside him. White people, to Okot, and also to Chip, were Paul's "tribe." His people had done this to Okot. Paul looked down and stirred the fire. He couldn't meet Okot's eyes.

"They's done that to all of us," Okot said. "Different marks for different owners. 'Cause we was sold. Then they started takin' us in canoes out to the big ship. My mother was taken too. There was black people from all differen' tribes, all chained together on the deck. So many I couldn't see 'em all. There was a great big fire burnin' inside a copper boiler. I thought that we was gonna get eaten by them white men.

"The women was separate from the men. I couldn't see nothin', but I could hear 'em, makin' sad songs the way they did in Nyamlel when someone died. So I thought, that's why they brung us here. They was gonna eat us."

"But white men don't do that!" Paul burst out.

Surprisingly, Okot grinned. "I didn' know that then. We couldn't think of nothin' else. But it was jus' a cookin' pot. For cookin' yams, not Dinka." He sighed. "The young boys wasn't chained. I thought they wasn't gonna chain me neither. But the crewmen kept lookin' an' pointin' at me, an' then they's chained me up next to a Dinka man. He was from a village near mine. He tol' me we wasn't gonna get eaten. We was goin' to the white men's country, to work for 'em. That made me feel better. But I kept lookin' through the nets that was all around the ship. Back at the land, an' the banana trees. I wanted to go home."

Paul and Chip nodded. They all wanted to go home. But Okot's home was much too far away. He could never go back.

"When the sun started goin' down," Okot went on, "they made us go down through a hole in the deck. We was chained up by our wrists and ankles, two men together. I didn' know where they took my mother, but the Dinka man said the women got a better place. He said the women didn' gotta be chained. So I's happy a bit for my mother."

"What was it like?" Paul asked. He remembered the ship he had come in from England with his father. It was huge, with wide wooden decks where they walked and watched the waves and the sky. They had a cabin with a little round porthole that they could open when the weather was fine.

"It was hard to see," Okot said. "Only a little bit o' light an' air comin' in. It was hot, an' it smelled like a dirty toilet." Okot felt sick just thinking about it. "The floor was slippery, with blood'n such stuff. There weren't hardly no room to move. There was planks along the walls, an' that took up most of the space. We had to lie down on'em, to make room for everyone."

Okot tried, but he couldn't describe to his new friends how terrible it had been. "We couldn' hardly breathe, it stunk so," he said. "An' through the walls we could hear the women and the little'uns yellin' an' cryin'. Then the hatch in the deck was banged shut. The ship was swayin' in the water. An' the chains rubbed somethin' awful."

Okot looked around their little shelter, with the cheerful fire, and he breathed in the fresh piney scents of the spruce and cedar branches they were sitting on. "We was there for days'n days," he said. "Every mornin', they chained us on deck, an' we could see Africa, so close. Every day they brung more prisoners on board. When they was finally finished, they shoved us all down below in the middle'o the day. An' there was terrible bangin' an' clangin' noises, and then the ship starts movin' up'n down in the water.

"I was sick then," he said. "So's everybody else. 'Cause of the way the ship was rockin'. We could hear the water splashin' against the sides. So we's all sick, and it stunk even more terrible."

Okot remembered how he had wanted to cry. He could hear the wailing of the women, and he wished he could be with his mother. But he had told himself, "Monyjang don't cry!" He looked sadly from Chip to Paul. "All's I was thinkin' was that my father was killed dead, an' maybe my little sisters an' brothers was all alone back in Nyamlel. An' me an' my mother was bein' taken away from Africa. Away from home, in this stinkin' hole, across this salt lake to some white man's country on th'other side."

Chapter 15

The New World

For a little while, Okot stopped speaking. The only sound was the endless drumming of rain on the shelter, and the sputtering and cracking of wood on the fire.

Chip and Paul had been listening with their eyes wide. Now Chip sat up again, and he began carving a feather stick. His knife made a soft, rhythmic whispering as he scraped the wood. The sound reminded Okot of the waves lapping against the hull of the slave ship. After a few minutes, he went on with his story.

"Every mornin' they's chained us to the deck. We had a big tub o' food for everyone. Sometimes yams. An' some water. The crewmen made the women sing an' dance. We could hear 'em, but their songs was all sad. This got the sailors mad. They's wantin' happy songs all the time, but no one had no happy songs inside them. An' they made us get up an' walk around the deck, so's we could have exercise. But they never took off the chains, 'cept when a man was so sick they thought he was gonna die.

"Before it got dark they always put us below again. There was only two pots for toilets, for everybody. They's called them 'necessary pots' but they's not made right, an' sometimes men fell in. People started gettin' sick right away. They had fevers an' sores all over. Every mornin', we brung up the men who died in the night, an' the sailors threw'em into the ocean, jus' like they was nothin' more than slops from the kitchen." Okot scowled.

"Then I got sick," he said. "After more'n two moons of sailin'. They puts me on deck after than, without no chains. There was lots of other men too. Many died. But not me. That's when I got to learn some English, 'cause I listened all the time to them crewmen. Some of th'other captives knew English, cause they was caught by slave raiders many moons before they was taken to the ship. They had to come a long ways in canoes to where we was kept on the beach.

"They was hateful to each other, too," Okot added. "I mean, them English. Once, one o' the sick men with me got over to the side of the ship, an' he threw himself into the water. When the man they called Cap'n found out, he beats the crewman who was supposed to be watchin' us. Then th'other white men threw that crewman off the ship."

"White men hate white men?" Chip said. "Is strange tribe, white men."

"I guess they got traitors too," Okot said. "Anyways, we finally saw some land, so we guessed this was white man's country. It was an island place. Them English calls it Barbados. They took us to the land an' it was hard to walk. It was when we first come onto the ship in Africa. Like the ground was movin'."

Paul nodded. "I remember that too. I felt like that when we came from England. All sick and dizzy again."

Chip looked from Paul to Okot. "But ground not move," he said. "Only water move."

"Maybe," Okot said, "I'll take you to Africa when I go home. Then you'll see."

"You think go home?" Chip asked.

"It was a joke," Paul said impatiently. But he saw that Chip was going to ask, "What mean joke?" So he said quickly to Okot, "What happened next?"

"There was a slave market," Okot said. "In town, an' there was big crowds of white people. They done lots o' shoutin' an' they calls us "bucks" an' they calls the women "wenches." They put us in stalls like animals an' people with white gloves put their fingers in my mouth an' felt my arms an' legs again, jus' like on the beach in Africa." Okot swallowed hard, remembering. "I saw my mother," he said. "Till then I didn' know if she died or not. But she was alive. I called her."

Okot screwed his eyes up tight. He remembered all the sweaty bodies around him and the chain biting into his wrists. "I called her," he said. "But a white man hit me with a stick. But she heard me. She looked all around, an' then she saw me."

Okot remembered his mother wailing and crying when she saw him. She couldn't wipe away the tears, and they ran down her face and dripped off her chin, down to the dusty ground of the marketplace. "She was taken up onto a high box an' sold," Okot said. "I never saw her no more." He picked up a stick and poked the fire.

"But what happened to you?" Paul asked.

"A man bought me who owned merchant ships. We sailed to this place the white men called Virginia, in the New World."

"But you can't take slaves to Virginia," Paul said. "President Thomas Jefferson said so."

Okot looked at him sadly. "This man took me," he said. "He brung me in a fine carriage to Master Abbot. An' the next thing, Payne comes. He's the overseer that's in charge o' the slaves. An' Payne tells me I belongs to Master Abbot cause of bein' used to pay for somethin' called a 'debt.'"

All at once, Okot surprised Paul and Chip by snorting with laughter. "I jus' thought of that," he said. "Master Abbot must've been double mad when he found I's gone. His debt done run away. I wonder if'n he sent for Payne to whip that man from Barbados."

They sat in silence for a while. Finally, Okot spoke up again. He had been thinking about something ever since Paul came. He said, "Mrs. Abbot read all the time from a Bible. Times she read to me, an' asked me questions, but I never understood nuthin' about it. It used to make her cry. Can you tell me what it means?"

"Well," Paul said, "I'm a Christian, like my father. The Bible—"

Okot interrupted him. "Payne said they's all Christians on the plantation. But he was hateful. An' they said we's all had to be Christians, an' they did it by givin' us slaves new names. They called me Benjamin, to make me a Christian. I hate them!"

"Not everyone who says he's a Christian really is," Paul said. "Some people think they're Christians just because their parents were. Or because they go to church."

"We all had to go to church," Okot said. "Them white men called it Sabbath meetin' house. It was the house where Jesus lives."

"Well, going to church doesn't make you a Christian," Paul said. "Changing your name doesn't either. Jesus doesn't live in a building. He lives in here." He pointed to his chest. "In your heart."

"In your heart?" Okot frowned. "That's what Mandy said." He explained about Mandy and Elisha. "I tol' Mandy that I never saw her God Jesus Savior Lord. She said I had to see with my heart, not my eyes."

"She was right," Paul said. "Real Christians are kind, and forgiving, like Jesus."

"Mrs. Abbot was kind to me. But she still own slaves. That's not right. She showed me where the Bible says there ain't no slaves nor free men. But there is. She said there ain't no difference between people. But there is. Your Bible lies."

"No!" Paul shouted. "God's Word doesn't lie!"

Chip and Okot stared at him, astounded.

Paul thought a quick, silent prayer. Then he said, "God doesn't lie. Men make slaves. That's wrong. God calls it sin. He hates sin. There were even slaves back when the Bible was written. There's lots about slaves and masters in the Bible. What Mrs. Abbot read to you, that means God sees us all as equal. He loves us all the same."

Okot sighed. "That's jus' what Mandy said. But if Mrs. Abbot believes that, why's she own slaves?"

"Maybe," Paul said, "that's why she was always crying."

"Cryin' don' help."

"Maybe," Paul added, "you need to forgive her for being weak. If Jesus is in her heart, one day He'll show her she's wrong."

"I don' understand about Jesus. Mandy said He's God. You say He's in your heart. Who is He?"

"Jesus is God's Son. He came to earth as a baby. You know about Christmas. That's when we celebrate Jesus' birthday. When He grew up He was killed by bad people. People who went to church and said they loved God. But they killed Jesus. They nailed Him to a dead tree trunk with a branch across it. It was called a cross."

Okot's eyes were wide. "But why? Was Jesus bad too?"

"No. He never did anything bad. He never did anything wrong even by accident. He's perfect."

"Then why'd God let Him get killed?"

"God planned it. Jesus took the punishment for everything bad that we ever did. For all our sin, so that we don't have to be punished for it. So we can be free."

All at once Okot felt like crying. He thought about Mandy being whipped in his place after he escaped. He thought of all the days when he had curled up to sleep and wished something could take away the awful feeling he had, because he was free and Mandy was punished for him. Maybe this God Jesus Savior thing did make sense. "At home, in our tribe," he told Paul, "when someone did somethin' wrong, like killed someone, he's had to kill Mabior. The white bull. This make everything right with spirits again. Is that like what this Jesus done for us?"

Paul nodded. He felt his heart stir with excitement. Maybe Okot really was beginning to understand it all. "Except," he added, "God didn't just use a bull. He sacrificed Himself."

Okot frowned. "But how can Jesus live in your heart when He's dead?"

"Because He's God. Three days later after He died on the cross, He came back to life. No one can kill God. He makes people live and die."

Okot's face became hard. "Then God let the slave raiders kill my father."

Paul had no answer for that.

After a minute, Chip yawned. And suddenly they were all yawning. Okot's story had taken a long time to tell. They didn't know how late it was because the rain was still coming down and there were no stars in the sky.

They stretched out by the fire. But for a long time Okot lay with his eyes open. He was remembering Mrs. Abbot holding her Bible and saying, with tears in her eyes, "I think we're the ones who are wrong."

Chapter 16

Good Hunting

By the week after the big storm Proudfoot's wounds were well healed. The tough little paint horse hardly limped at all.

Paul had found out from Okot that he had never ridden a horse, even though he had learned how to handle them at the Abbots' plantation. So, each morning and afternoon, he gave him a riding lesson on Storm. Okot rode bareback, so that he would be able to ride behind Chip or Paul when they started to travel. He was so strong and graceful that he learned quickly. Proudfoot followed Storm and Okot around the clearing when they had their lessons.

Once Proudfoot was walking soundly, Chip began riding along beside Okot. The long gouges that the bear had made in his leg were healed now, but underneath the puckered scars his muscles were still torn and weak. His leg had twisted as it healed, and he walked with an odd rolling gait. He worked hard at stretching and strengthening the muscles, by swimming in the stream and by riding every day. Soon, he thought, he would be ready for the long ride back home.

While they rode around the clearing, they often talked about how their fathers had taught them to live in the wilderness. Chip's English got better every day, and Paul began thinking to himself, if he can learn English, I can learn Iroquois. He decided that, when he got back to his father, he would make a real effort to study Chip's language.

One day after the morning lesson, when Paul and Okot were cleaning the trout that Chip had shot for lunch, Okot suddenly said, "Paul, you gonna be a preacher man when you grow up, like your father?"

"I always thought I would be," he said. "But now, I like this kind of life." He waved his arm around the clearing. "Some days, I think I'd like to be a hunter or a trapper, and always live out in the open. Go on long hunting trips, like Chip."

Chip, coming up behind them, overheard this. "Must be very brave," he said. "To live like these trappers. Is very dangerous. And in nights of the long moons, many white men die, from cold and snow and wolves."

"Wolverines, too?" Paul asked, grinning.

"Them too," Chip agreed. "You must be very quick with bow and arrow, and knife."

Paul whipped out his knife and tossed it high in the air. It turned end over end, and he caught it easily. "Quick like that?" he asked.

"Like this!" Chip said, pulling out his own knife and slashing it through the air. Paul jumped to his feet, and he and Chip fenced with each other. The clearing rang with the clinking of metal. Then they both tossed their knives. Sunshine glinted off the blades.

Okot, who couldn't play that way with his little kitchen knife, went off to do one of his favorite things—climb a tree and swing from the branches by his knees. Paul pointed to him and said to Chip, "Can you hit the middle of that tree?"

"Aarrgh!" Okot shouted, jumping to the ground. "So, white man gonna let Onondaga kill me?"

Paul laughed. "Nah. Chip couldn't hit that place."

Okot ran to join them, and Chip took careful aim. Whoosh! The knife flew out of his hand, straight to the tree trunk. The sharp point bit into the bark with a soft thud.

"Not quite the middle," Paul said, trying not to be too impressed. "See?" He threw his knife, and it stuck into the bark above Chip's, right in the center.

"If that was deer, not tree, you shoot neck," Chip said. "I shoot heart, like good hunter. My hit was better."

Okot held his knife in his hands. It wasn't heavy enough for hunting or throwing. But he had to take his turn. He narrowed his eyes, and then he threw the puny knife as hard as he could. There was a clang, and it bounced off the others.

"Is good throw," Chip said generously. "You not have good knife." He trotted over to pick up all three of the knives. He hardly limped at all now. Chip handed Paul's knife back. Then, after a minute, he held out his own knife to Okot. "Here. Throw this."

Okot balanced the knife carefully. It felt good in his hand, a good weapon, like a spear. But it felt best because Chip had given it to him. Just like that. He smiled, and threw it, hard and straight, at the tree. It hit right on Chip's mark.

"Aiee!" Chip shouted, and danced in a little circle, whooping and hollering. "We all braves. We have killed a big buck. Now we must cut it. Then we have good meat to eat."

They laughed, but the thought of roasting venison reminded them of how hungry they were. "Just fish today," Chip said, sighing, as they walked back to the stream. "Soon we hunt buck."

That afternoon, Okot asked Chip something he'd wanted to ever since they met. "Chip, will you teach me to shoot an arrow?"

Chip had never yet let either Paul or Okot shoot his bow. It was always slung over his shoulder, or ready in his hands. He was squatting by the shelter, making feather sticks, when Okot asked him. He hesitated for a long moment. His bow was the most valuable thing he owned. Even more important than his knife. But suddenly he smiled. "Aiee!" he shouted. "Is great idea. Then I can rest sometimes, and black brave can shoot supper."

First, Chip marked out a target on a wide maple tree trunk with a piece of charred wood from the fire. Then he showed Okot how to grasp the bow, bending his bow arm slightly. He showed Okot the nock on the arrow, and how to fit it on the string. Then he guided Okot's arm as he drew it back, increasing the tension on the bow. "This bow too small for you. You Monyjang is all long arms and legs. But we try. Now, you must look only at this target. Imagine, is big buck. You must be still like stone. Not scare him, or we not have meat for supper." He stood back and studied the position of Okot's body, and the aim of his arrow. "Is good," he nodded approvingly. "Shoot now."

Just as Okot released the arrow, there was a soft nickering behind them, and Storm pushed his muzzle into Okot's back. The arrow flew wide of the target, rushing instead through the leafy branches and smacking into a notch high overhead.

"Arrgh!" Okot cried in frustration. It had looked so easy whenever Chip shot an arrow. It didn't seem to matter how he moved—he never missed his target.

Paul laughed, and shoved Storm away. "Go on, you old cow," he said. "Or they'll make *you* the target."

"It's okay," Chip told Okot. "Was only first try." Okot swung up into the tree and retrieved the arrow. When he was ready to try again, Chip reminded him, "No matter what happen. Horse, or maybe only bee buzz by. You must keep eyes only on big buck. Not look at arrow. Not anywhere but at buck. See mark on tree. Draw back string. Let go."

Once more Okot focused on the target. He held his breath and released the arrow. Zing! This time it flew straight and true, hitting the tree a few inches below the target.

"Good! Good!" Chip and Paul both cried. "Now shoot next, quick, before wounded buck run away!" Chip added.

Okot practiced all afternoon. Paul lay back on his elbows beside Chip, chewing a blade of grass and watching. When Okot finally had to put down the bow, because his arms were aching with tiredness, Paul looked at it longingly.

Chip saw this and his eyes narrowed. *I should let him shoot too,* he thought. But he couldn't imagine letting a white man hold the bow of an Onondaga brave. He could almost hear what Thunder Arm would say: "You are not my son. You are a traitor to our Hotahyonhne clan, and to the Onondaga." But Paul was his friend. What was the difference between him and Okot using the bow?

Suddenly Chip decided. He picked up the bow, and his quiver of arrows, and held them out to Paul. "You want to learn too?"

Paul jumped up eagerly, his face flushed red. He knew how hard it was for Chip to trust him this way. He took the bow, grinning, and fitted an arrow on the string. He tested the tension in his hands, and then, taking careful aim, drew back the arrow and let it fly. It hit just high and to the left of the target.

Chip and Okot gasped. "You know how to shoot!" Chip said accusingly. "Why you not say so?"

"I know a little," Paul said. "A friend taught me. He was a great archer. We used to have contests all the time. You know, to see who was the best."

"Aiee! Yes!" Chip shouted. "We do this contest also."

"After I get more practice," Okot said. He took the bow and arrows from Paul, and went back to shooting by himself. He felt left out. Paul and Chip could do so many things better than he could—riding and shooting and knife throwing—and they had friends and fathers too. For a minute he felt like he had back on the slave ship, when he was only eleven years old, and he missed his mother and father so much. Fiercely he put those thoughts out of his head and concentrated on his shooting.

A few yards away Paul and Chip sat back down on the grass. Chip picked up a small branch and began peeling it to make another feather stick. "Paul," he said after a while, "why you said you don't have this contests no more with your friend?"

Paul took the blade of grass out of his mouth. "Because he's dead," he said. "He was killed in an Indian massacre.

Killed and scalped. With all his family, and the other settlers."

For a long time Chip didn't speak. He just sat there, staring into the distance. Finally, he said, "Why you not hate me? Hate all Haudenosaunee?"

Paul looked up at his new friend. Chip's voice was different—quiet and sad. Paul said, "I did, when it first happened. I was arguing about it with my father just before we were separated. I said all Indians were murderers. Killers. But I know it's not true. There are bad Indians and bad white men." He glanced over at Okot. "Bad black men too. Only God can make things right."

"You mean this Jesus God?"

"Yes. That's why He's called our Savior. He saves us from all those bad things. He makes us want to do good things."

"But it good thing to kill white men when they make Great Spirit angry."

Paul shook his head. "It's never right to kill people."

"Hey!" Okot shouted at them suddenly. "I's ready now. Time for our first contest!"

Paul and Chip scrambled to their feet. Both were glad to stop talking.

They started shooting at all kinds of targets. "That leaf!" Chip shouted, pointing to a single red maple leaf dangling from one of the lower branches. Okot shot first. His arrow arced high and brushed past the leaf to lodge in the big branch behind. Paul's arrow tore through one side of the leaf. Chip's took the leaf dead in the center, and curved back down to earth.

They shot at the whispering birch trees, and then at fat clumps of bright orange berries on a bushy tree that Paul said was called a rowan. They searched in the stream for fish. Paul shot a trout in the tail, and Okot finished it off with his knife on the bank. Then it was his turn.

He waited patiently, up to his waist in water, as he had so often seen Chip do. His heart was thumping, and in spite of the chill of the stream his fingers were slippery with sweat. He felt the way he used to when his father watched him throw a spear. The first trout he saw was a great long one, swimming upstream near the far bank. Okot loosed his arrow, but it hit the water above the fish, and splashed harmlessly up against the grass. He learned from that how much the water bent the light, and he changed his aim so that, the next time, he shot a trout right behind the gills. He jumped after it, quick as a rabbit, and held up the arrow triumphantly with his wriggling catch on the end of it. "Aiee!" he shouted. "Hey, Onondaga brave, what you think of that?"

"Is so small it can be for your supper!" Chip shouted back. But he grinned, and Paul jumped into the stream and leaped on Okot's shoulders, howling with delight.

By the time it began to grow dark they were all tired of shooting. Chip was undoubtedly the champion but Paul and Okot didn't mind too much. "If'n you spent all the time I's had to spend pickin' tobacco, you wouldn't be no good at bow shootin' neither," Okot said.

Paul flung himself on the grass, panting. "And if you'd spent your life traveling with a preacher man like my father, you wouldn't be so good either."

"Too bad," Chip said, taking out his knife and slitting open one of the trout. "You not been born Onondaga braves."

"Someday I'm gonna take you to Africa," Okot said. "Then I'm gonna show you how Monyjang hunt."

"Right now, it's good how we all hunt," Paul said, taking out his knife. "We've got three good trout for supper."

Every morning, as soon as he woke up, Chip spent a few minutes studying the trees and the sky. All the summer green was gone now on the oaks and maples and birch trees. The leaves were bright yellow and orange and scarlet, and some of them were already starting to fall. The nights were cold, and every morning there was a heavy white dew on the grass. Overhead, geese filled the sky with their honking. He thought back to what the trapper had said, and Thunder Arm's warning about an early winter. *It's time,* he thought. *We can't stay here much longer.*

One particularly frosty morning Chip finally said to the others, "We must shoot deer. We can dry the meat. For the trip home." He pointed to the colored leaves in the trees. "The moon of harvest is almost gone. The long cold moons come. We must ride to find where deer eat. Then I stay. I shoot good buck."

That afternoon, Paul and Chip rode off together on Storm. Okot had to hold on tightly to Proudfoot until they were out of sight. The little paint whinnied frantically for Storm, stomping his hooves and tossing his head furiously at being kept back.

It was getting dark by the time Okot heard the soft thudding of Storm's hooves again in the clearing. He came out of the shelter, where he had been building up the fire, and Proudfoot nickered hello.

Chip had shot a rabbit for supper, and Paul had filled one of his saddlebags with hazelnuts. They were tired and thirsty and scratched up from the branches they'd had to push through in the woods. "But we found a good place," Paul said, as he pulled the saddle off Storm. "Fresh deer droppings, and good grass."

"Good hiding place," Chip added. "We go tonight, when moon come up."

Okot cleaned and skewered the rabbit, and set it to roast over the fire. Chip lay down to rest his sore leg, and Paul helped him put fresh feathers in his arrows. They didn't say much as they ate. Finally, Paul said what they were all thinking. "This hunting trip means we're nearly ready to leave. If we get a deer."

"We go home," Chip said. "To my village. To Paul's home."

"This is my home," Okot said suddenly. "This is the only home I got, since they took me away from Africa."

Paul thought back to when he and his father had come on the great ship from England. He had no idea then what his new home would be like. But it was all right, because he was with his father. But Okot had no one. *I'll have to take care of him,* Paul said to himself. *My father would want me to.*

Paul and Chip set off again when the moon shone high and bright above the trees. It seemed to Okot that he waited a long time alone in the dark before Paul came riding back by himself. "Chip said that if he shoots a buck, he'll make a shout like a blue jay," he told Okot. "He says that we should be able to hear him. Then we can go back to help."

"You think he's all right?" Okot said. "His leg was worse tonight."

"It's all cramped up from riding," Paul said. "But he's used to hunting like this. Anyway, all we can do is pray."

"Pray," Okot repeated. "You mean to his Great Spirit? Or to your Jesus God?"

"To Jesus," Paul said. "I told you there's no Great Spirit. Not like Chip believes. There's only one real God. Jesus."

Okot's eyes widened, and he looked around the clearing fearfully. "Paul, Chip said you gonna make the Great Spirit angry talkin' like that. Something bad's gonna go wrong for us."

"Not if we pray," Paul said. He closed his eyes, and turned away. Okot knew he was praying to his God. He looked out, up at the stars. All the night sounds of the forest came loud to his ears. The branches of the trees seemed to moan in the wind. He thought he could see eyes shining through the darkness from the woods. Creatures he didn't know the names of twittered and rustled in the undergrowth. *Danger*, everything seemed to whisper. Okot shivered. He tried to think of the Jesus God that Mandy had told him about, but all he could imagine was the Great Spirit that Chip said owned this land. Okot almost thought he could hear a voice from the sky telling him, *Danger, Okot. This is not your country.*

A piercing shout startled Okot awake. He and Paul had both fallen asleep on the grass. They shook themselves and stood up stiffly. Morning was breaking, and the grass was wet and white with dew. The shout came again. Paul said, "That's Chip! He must have got a deer!"

When Paul had left and Chip was alone, he settled himself in a thicket at the edge of the feeding yard. He knew he had at least two or three hours to wait until any deer would approach the little glade. They were shy creatures, and anything unusual would keep them away. A sound, a scent, even a broken branch. He would have to sit without moving a muscle, hardly even breathing, until he had a clear shot at a buck. Even then, it would be so easy to miss.

Chip licked his lips, and drew out an arrow to have ready on the string. "O Great Spirit," he prayed, "make my hunting successful tonight. Let me be a true son of my clan. Make my arrow quick and straight in flight, so that I may kill this buck like the wolf, because I am a son of the Hotahyonhne clan."

The first deer came in the shadows of predawn, so silently that Chip was not sure at first if they were only there in his imagination. He blinked, carefully, and strained his eyes. A doe, with two spotted fawns.

Chip waited. His wounded leg was cramped up, and felt full of hot knives. But he did not move.

When the young buck glided into the open, it was behind the fawns, and Chip couldn't get a clear shot. Then the buck raised its head, alerted by some movement or scent. It was ready to run. Chip loosed an arrow. Twang! The shaft flew straight and true. It hit the buck behind its foreleg. In a flash, Chip followed it with another. This time, he was able to draw the bow as tight as it would go. This arrow went in beside the first, but deeper, almost to the flight. The buck took a few steps, staggering. Chip shot a third arrow, and the buck was down, on its side.

"Aiee!" he shouted, breaking the silence of the woods. He sent out his piercing blue jay shriek for Paul and Okot. Then he kneeled beside the dying buck, pulling his knife from its sheath. "Great Spirit," he prayed, "give Thunder Arm a vision to see me now. I am an Onondaga brave!"

Chip had already cut the buck when Paul and Okot reached him. The blood was running out of the meat and pooling on the pine needles of the forest floor. Paul and

Okot swung down off the horses. "Good hunting, my brave!" Paul cried.

Chip grinned, thumping himself on the chest. "Aiee! Yes!" he yelled. "Onondaga brave!" He did a little war dance, holding his bow high over his head. But he was clumsy, because his sore leg was so stiff. He tripped over his own feet, and fell next to the buck. "Ugh!" he shouted, throwing aside his bow. "Maybe next time I shoot bear that hurt me."

"Better we don't see a bear now," Paul said. "It would eat all of us." He got out his knife, and he and Chip got down to carving up the meat. They worked quickly as the sun came up, skinning the deer and carving out the great haunches and shoulders. By the time they finished the messy job they were filthy with sweat and blood. It was getting warm, and flies buzzed all around them.

Chip was unhappy about leaving behind the buck's hide. He satisfied himself by cutting several long thin strips of hide with his knife. "Makes good strong ties," he explained, jamming them under his belt. None of them knew just how important those pieces of deer hide were going to be.

They wiped their hands as clean as they could, on the outside of the dead buck's hide. Then they cleaned their knives by wiping them on the pine needles. Paul had brought his oilskin, and Okot helped him load the meat onto it. Paul made a big pouch by gathering up the edges of the oilskin, and then he slung it up and over Storm's withers. He and his horse had both done this many times. Storm stood like a soldier and didn't even roll his eyes at the smelly load he was carrying.

"White man make good brave soon," Chip said. "White horse make good hunter too."

Paul felt warm and satisfied at Chip's praise. He swung up on Storm's back, behind the load of venison. Okot gave Chip a leg up onto Proudfoot, and then leaped up behind him. Together they set off back to their clearing.

The first thing Chip and Paul did was to jump in the stream to have a good wash. They rushed into the water, whooping and laughing. Okot pulled off Storm's saddle and set the meat down on the bank. They were all excited, because it was the first time they had killed and cleaned a buck by themselves. But Okot felt left out, because he didn't have a good knife and hadn't done much to help.

Paul picked up a handful of stones and tossed one upstream. It whirled and shone in the sun, and skipped over the surface of the water. "Wham!" he shouted, and did it again. "Wham! Wham! What a great shot, Chip! First time! Three arrows. One big buck."

"See that?" Okot said, pointing way upstream, to where a line of rocks broke the surface of the water. "Who can hit that? The biggest buck of all!"

Paul and Chip tried. The water churned as stones landed all around the rocks, but none of them seemed to hit the dark rock in the middle. Finally Okot laughed. "You can't," he said. "It ain't a rock. It's just a shadow."

The others didn't believe him, so they waded up the stream to find out. Okot was right. They came back to him, amazed. "How did you know?" Paul asked. "It still looks like a rock from here."

"I am Monyjang," Okot said. "Monyjang got the best eyes in all Africa."

Paul shook his head. "I guess so."

Okot whipped a stone upstream. It landed with a sharp smack right in the middle of the black shadow. Paul whistled, and Okot felt a little better.

Chip had told Paul and Okot that in the cold of winter the Onondaga hung venison in the air to dry. But now it was not cold enough, and the flies would lay their eggs in it and make it rot. So they had to smoke it dry.

The first thing they did was take a haunch of venison back to the shelter to roast over the fire. While it cooked, Paul and Okot began to carve the rest of the meat into thick strips. Okot had to stop often to sharpen his little kitchen knife.

Meanwhile, Chip cut young green branches from the clump of birch trees, and wove them into a square rack. "Now we get good green leaves," he said, "and make smoke place." He built up the fire on the bank of the stream, and they all went looking for rocks to make a stand for the birch rack. They gathered hickory branches and leaves to make the fire smoky, and then they laid the strips of venison on the rack over the fire.

"How long does it take?" Okot asked, looking about him. The breeze had grown stronger, and there was a strange kind of light in the sky. The light before a storm.

Chip looked at the way the leaves of the birch and maple trees were turning up into the wind. He nodded, frowning. "Big storm come," he said at last. "Maybe first storm of the cold moons. Trees know. Birds too." He was listening to the worried twittering of the songbirds, and the redwings that trilled without stopping. "Is okay, I think. Meat be dry before it comes."

"The homesteaders smoke it dry in just a few hours," Paul told Okot. "It'll be done before tonight."

Chip filled Paul's tin cooking pot with water, and added some of his precious salt to it. Then he put the long strips of deer hide in to soak. "I wet hide, then scrape and scrape and scrape," he told the others. "It take many moons for making hide for clothes. But this ropes be good for our long trip."

That night, when the dried venison was safely packed away in Paul's saddlebags, ready for their journey, they heard wolves howling in the woods. "Is bad sign," Chip said, putting another big branch on the fire in their shelter. "Winter moons soon be here. Wolves not bad for people. But bad for horses. We must be careful. Not let fire stop."

What about when we start out for Ohsweken? Okot thought. What about the wolves then? But he kept his thoughts to himself.

Chapter 17

The Pact

In the next few days the three of them rode further and further away from the clearing, getting the horses used to more exercise, and getting themselves used to being on horseback for several hours at a time. The scars on Chip's twisted leg were deep and long and purple, but the skin was all healed. He did not have as many cramps even after riding for two or three hours.

On each trip one of them took the bow and arrows, and they shot rabbits and geese to eat. Okot killed two small rattlesnakes one day with Paul's knife, and they roasted the snake meat in a little glade deep in the forest. Paul and Chip kept the rattles, so now they each had one. Each rattle made a slightly different sound as it dried, and in a couple of days they could tell each other in the dark by the sound of their rattles.

The nights now were long, clear and cold. The boys studied the stars together, and from the North Star they marked out the direction they would take when they finally set out on their trip back.

One day, near the place where the trapper had camped, Chip found some plants growing up through the dank leaves on the forest floor that made him leap off Proudfoot and jump up and down with excitement. "Is plant with blood roots!" he cried. "Is for war paint. Is for making blood color on braves!"

Okot, sitting behind Paul on Storm, felt the white boy shudder. He was afraid himself. What did Chip want with war paint?

Chip was already pulling up big handfuls of the bloodroot plant. Back at the clearing, he cut the roots, and the sap ran out into Paul's tin cooking pot, just like a river of fresh blood. "We can color buck," Chip said, as though Paul and Okot should know exactly what he was talking about.

Every day since they had killed the buck, Chip had scraped his strips of hide, and then left them to smoke on the drying rack. Now, he took one of the strips and dunked it in the red sap. "Tomorrow," he said, "we have red rope."

"But why do we want it red?" Paul asked sensibly.

"No reason," Chip admitted. "Except it talk to me of home. We can dress us up for when we go home, with this." His eyes glowed with excitement as he struggled to explain. "Then the braves know we not just lost. They know we lived like wise braves in forest. Thunder Arm be proud of me. My mother's eyes shine." The next day he pulled the deerskin, now dyed a deep scarlet, out of its bath, and hung it back on the rack to smoke dry.

There had been no sign of the man who had robbed the French trapper. "Him be gone long time," Chip said. "Him sell them beaver pelts at the trading post. No one know he steal them." But they still tied the horses up each night outside the shelter, just in case.

They left the clearing for good on the morning of the first snow. Only a few flakes had fallen in the night, but Okot was still fascinated. He scrambled out of the shelter before it was light, and scuffled his bare feet in the snow. But soon the cold drove him back inside.

Chip had stirred the fire and thrown on a couple of small logs to get the flames crackling again. They huddled around it and ate the rest of the roasted goose Paul had shot the day before. They were each busy with their own thoughts, and they ate in silence. When they had finished, they saddled up Storm, and loaded him with the bulging saddlebags.

Paul placed his few possessions on his bedroll: the rest of the salt, his flint and steel, and his Bible. He rolled up the bedroll tightly with these inside, and wrapped it in the oilskin. He tied it to the back of his saddle, and was ready to go. Suddenly, he remembered how he had done this with his father, early in the morning of the day that they were separated. *In ten days, maybe less,* he thought, *I'll know if he is dead or alive.* He shivered—from anticipation and from fear.

Storm stood patiently, as he had been taught, when Paul left him and joined the others in the shelter again.

They could only just see each other in the dim light of the fire. *It's strange,* Paul thought, *to be so excited and so scared at the same time.* What would happen to them in the next few days? What would he do, if he found out that he was left all alone in the world?

This was my home, Okot thought, looking around the little shelter. *The best home since Nyamlel. What am I going to do now?*

Chip didn't have any such fears. He knew he was going home. It might take many days' riding, but he would find Ohsweken again, and his mother and brothers and sister would be there, waiting for him. And Thunder Arm would be proud of his youngest son, who had survived a bear charge, and killed a buck, and found his way back to the village. But, in spite of what he had said to Paul and Okot about their being welcomed as his friends, Chip knew deep down that Thunder Arm would be angry with him. There was no telling what he would do with Paul and Okot.

Suddenly Paul said, "This is like leaving my home in England again. We didn't know what was going to happen in the New World. But my father promised that he would take care of me, and that we would always be together. He said that the two of us, with God helping, made a threefold cord. And the Bible says that a threefold cord is strong and so it's not easy to break." He stopped. He was a bit embarrassed, because the other two were silent. But he went on. "So, I thought, we don't know what's going to happen now. But the three of us—if we promise to stick together—we make a strong cord." He swallowed. "Right?"

Chip thought, *Paul's talking about his white man's God again.* But he understood about the cord. He knew how to braid three strips of deerskin to make a strong rope. He said, "Right," very seriously.

Okot looked from one to the other. *We might not be able to stay together,* he thought. *But at least if we promise to try, it might be better.* He smiled, and his white teeth flashed in the gray light. "Yes. We'll make a promise."

Chip said, "This mean we be like braves in war. We must fight for each other."

"A pact," Paul said. "We'll make a pact to be like brothers."

"Funny brothers," Okot laughed. "Black, white, and brown."

"Brothers under the skin," Paul said. "We all have the same color blood."

"Blood brothers!" Chip said.

"Better than friends," Okot added.

"No matter what happens," Paul agreed. "We should have something to remind us."

"A cord," Okot said. "Like you said. A—threefold? Is that right?"

"I can make this," Chip said. "I make from buck. One cord from three." He went outside, and came back with the long narrow thongs of deerskin. He sorted out from them two of the plain strips, and one that he had dyed red with the weird bloodroot plant. "This for us blood brothers," he said, holding it up. Swiftly he braided it with two of the undyed strips. "What call this, Paul?"

"In England we called it a plait," he said. "But sometimes here it's called a braid."

"Braid. Yes." Chip wrapped the braided throngs around Paul's wrist. It took him only a minute to cut the cord to the right length and tie it off. "Now Okot," he said, and did the same thing.

Okot watched as Chip braided together the ends of the deerskin, and saw that the thongs covered up the scars on his wrist from the chains that he had worn for so long. He grinned at Chip and Paul. "Just like the chains them slavers put on me," he said. "But this is a chain of friends." The hide looked almost white next to his black skin, and the red thong braided into the middle looked like a river of flame.

It's like belonging to God, Paul wanted to say. A slave to Jesus, instead of to men. *Maybe,* he thought excitedly, *this really is why God brought us together.* He took the last length of braided hide, and wound it around Chip's wrist, tying it the way Chip had shown him. Chip held out his wrist with the deerskin braid. "Blood brothers," he said.

Paul crossed his wrist over Chip's. "Friends forever," he said.

Okot crossed his wrist over Paul's. They stayed like that, with the firelight flickering on their faces and in their eyes as they looked solemnly from one to the other. They were thinking of the many things that could break them apart in the next few days. "Friends and brothers," Okot said firmly. "No matter what happens."

They rode far to the north that day, following the direction they had marked out by studying the North Star, and then doing their best to keep on course by the sun. That night they camped in the open, in a small forest glade where a fresh spring gushed out from the side of a small rocky bluff. The wind moaned through the trees overhead, but they didn't dare light a fire. It was lonely and uncomfortable after the warmth of their shelter in the clearing.

Storm had brushed through a thorn bush earlier in the day, and Paul looked at his scratches with Chip. "Is much bleeding," Chip said, "but I think not very bad."

They let the horses have a good roll on the coarse brown grass, and then hobbled them for the night. "I made supper in our house," Okot said jokingly, when Chip and Paul joined him. He had made a rough bed of cedar boughs, covered with the oilskin, and laid out their dried venison on it. The cooking pot was heaped with nuts and berries.

They wrapped themselves up in Paul's bedroll while they ate. The night was so clear that the stars seemed bigger and brighter than normal. They could see their breath, and their lungs ached with the cold. When they lay down, huddled together for warmth, Chip told a story of how the gift of fire came to the Haudenosaunee, from a boy who had a vision on his dream fast. "In two years, I go on my dream fast," he added. "And then the Great Spirit will tell me what my animal guide will be."

"But what if the Great Spirit don't tell you?" Okot asked.

"This happen sometimes," Chip said sadly. "Then is bad. Is big shame. I never be brave then."

"You'll always be brave," Paul said. "Does this thing matter so much?"

"This mean everything!" Chip exclaimed. "It make me a man."

Paul said, "God makes men."

"You says this because white man never be able to do dream fast," Chip said scornfully. "White men not strong like braves."

They had trouble sleeping that night. Part of it was the cold. Every time one of them moved a draft of icy air struck them on the neck or back or feet. And part of it was the tension between Paul and Chip.

A gibbous moon lit the glade with bright cold light. Paul had given up trying to sleep, which was why he was the first to see the gray shadows gliding at the edge of the woods. At that moment the horses snorted and stamped with restless fear.

Chip woke immediately and reached for his bow. Paul was already crouching with his knife in his hand when the wolves charged at the horses. He only had time to think, *It's because of the blood from Storm's scratches,* before his horse gave a terrified scream. Storm tried to run, but the hobbles stopped him and he fell. A wolf leaped for his throat! Paul didn't realize he was screaming too as he ran to Storm.

"Paul, stop!" Okot cried. "They'll kill you!"

An arrow whizzed past Paul's head. One of the wolves yelped and turned back to the woods. But the lead wolf was on Storm's neck. The horse kicked violently with his hind legs, but with his forelegs hobbled he was helpless. Paul threw himself over Storm's shoulders, jabbing with his knife. The wolf snarled and snapped. Now it had a grip on the pulsing underside of Storm's jaw. Any second it would bite through, and Storm's blood would spurt out in a great fountain.

The wild terror in Storm's eyes robbed Paul of fear. He launched himself in fury at the wolf, slashing and lunging with his knife. Dimly he was aware of another arrow flying by. He felt claws scraping his skin. He pulled back his arm, and plunged his knife deep, deeper into the throat of the wolf. The wolf turned on him, but already the life was going out of it. With all his strength, Paul twisted the knife in its throat. The wolf staggered, and sank down on its side.

Snorting and whinnying, Storm struggled to his feet. Paul lay on the grass, still holding his knife. It was Okot who pried his fingers off the knife and helped him to his feet.

Paul stumbled and nearly fell over again. "What happened?" he asked dazedly.

"You kill lead wolf," Chip said. He was awestruck. "You must be messenger of the Great Spirit."

Paul laughed shakily. "No, no. I was just mad. My father gave me Storm. I couldn't let him be eaten by a wolf. I promised I would take care of him."

"We must take hide," Chip said, looking around for a rock to sharpen his knife. "You are white brave. Wolf now be your guide."

The ghostly light of the moon fell on a strange sight in the glade that night. The horses, peaceful again, grazing quietly by the little stream. And three young men, in filthy tattered clothes, crouching over the body of a timber wolf. Chip worked more carefully than he would if he were only skinning an animal for them to eat. He slit the wolf all along the underside, and then began peeling back the hide, separating it from the wolf's flesh. His hands were skillful, and Paul and Okot watched amazed as he showed them how he eased the thin hide off the wolf's skull.

The sun was up by the time Chip finished. He turned the hide over on the grass, and then Paul, using the flat of his knife blade, scraped away the last bits of flesh that clung to it. Then he carried it to the spring, and washed and scraped the flesh side of the hide again. Okot, still amazed at what Paul had done, hung the wolf hide over a tree branch to dry while Paul and Chip washed themselves.

Okot, looking at the mess they had left on the grass, pointed to the wolf's carcass. "What do we do with that?"

"Leave it," Chip said unconcernedly. "It be eat up soon as we gone." He grinned. "Wolverine can have this time, instead of white man's shoulder."

Paul laughed. "What a lot's happened since we met," he said, thinking back to their first night together.

When the hide was dry enough, Paul slung it across the front of his saddle, and lashed in on with a couple of the deerskin thongs.

Chip was watching him, and he said suddenly, "Paul, I'm sorry I said white men aren't brave."

"That's okay," Paul said, tightening the girth and turning around. "If I were brave, I wouldn't be here. It's because I was a coward that I lost my father." It was a relief finally to say it out loud.

"We find him again," Chip said. He held up his arm with the wrist braid. "Brother."

Okot, walking toward them from the edge of the glade, couldn't hear what they were saying. But he could see their smiles, and he breathed a loud sigh of relief, knowing everything was all right again. "You got your first hide," he said to Paul when he reached them. "Maybe your God is tellin' you to be a trapper, instead of a preacher man."

"Hey!" Paul exclaimed. "If only Giant John could see me now. Then he wouldn't ever laugh at me again."

"Giant John?" Chip asked. "Him big white man trapper?"

"You know him?"

"Yeah. Him big friend of Ohsweken. Him save my brother Swift Deer. After winter moons, when Great Spirit breathe on ice in Onondaga river, you know is time to be careful. Onondaga river have strong spirit. Very fast current. But Swift Deer always make contest with spirits. Him was fishing when hard water broke under him. River spirit pull him down, and rocks make big hole in his head. But Giant John saw him and leaps in river like big fish. Is big fight with spirit in river, but him give up Swift Deer, give him back to us. Giant John sick with fever then, and stay in our longhouse one moon. Now him good friend."

Paul listened in amazement. He remembered now that there had been weeks back in the early spring when no one had seen Giant John, and many people wondered if he had been mauled by another bear, or killed by wolves, alone somewhere in the bush. When he did show up, he didn't say a word about where he had been, and no one thought anything of it, because he came and went as he pleased. Now, Paul was surprised that he hadn't boasted about saving an Indian brave's life. But then, people already called him an "Indian lover" and they weren't nice when they said it. Maybe even a big mouth like John Grant knew when it was better to keep his mouth shut.

Or maybe, Paul thought as he swung up into his saddle behind the wolf hide, *maybe he's not as bad a man as we all think he is.*

Chapter 18
A New Master

Over the next few days Okot thought often about Paul and his Jesus Lord Savior God. Chip seemed to be afraid of his Great Spirit god. And Okot's father used to talk about the spirits of his ancestors, but he never knew if they were going to fight on the side of his tribe, or another, whether they would be helpful or cruel. He was always sacrificing Mabior to the spirits and his dead family. Yet when Paul talked about his Jesus, he was never afraid. He talked to the Jesus God as though He was a friend, not a spirit that might be angry.

When Okot mulled this over in his mind, he had a strange, tight feeling in his chest. But it was a warm kind of feeling, like a fire on a dark cold night. Like the way Paul described the cozy feeling to Chip. When that thought came to Okot, he looked around guiltily. Maybe he shouldn't think that way about a god, even Paul's God. So he put it out of his mind, and thought instead about trying to convince Chip that they should try to shoot a rabbit or something else for supper. He was getting sick of eating nothing but dried venison.

They went through thick forests and across old trails. Sometimes they came out to broad grassy meadows, and they stopped to rest and let the horses graze. They forded streams and pushed their way through thickets of hawthorn. Paul told them the English names of the trees and wildflowers, and Chip told them the words in his language. Okot and Paul struggled to repeat what he said, but the strange long names made their mouths gum up with spit, and they always ended up snorting with laughter at each other.

On the edges of woods they saw squirrels, and occasionally fox or deer in the distance. Early in the mornings, and late in the evenings as they prepared to camp for the night, they saw porcupines, and many raccoons chattering high in the trees. They thought longingly of having hot roasted meat again.

Once, Okot smelt something strange that made him wrinkle up his nose. "I didn't know you had zorillas here," he said. "Ugh!"

"That stink!" Paul said, plugging his nose. "That's a skunk, Okot."

Chip, speaking over his shoulder, told them about how his dog had once been sprayed by a skunk, when it was just a pup. It had whined and howled and skulked through the whole village with its tail drooping between its legs. The women threw pebbles at it and chased it outside the palisade, waving cornstalks and banging their pots. Okot and Paul laughed until their sides hurt. "Him smelled bad for two moons," Chip said. "I wash him all the time, but it not help."

For five days they didn't see anyone. In the afternoon of the sixth day they came to an area of low hills and valleys. They rode up many of the hills, searching in the distance for smoke that would mean village fires. At last they came to a large cleared area of land, with a few yellowed stalks still standing here and there like tired soldiers. "Cornfield," Chip said, and the others heard the excitement in his voice. They rested there, and let the horses snuffle the ground for dried corn kernels. Chip and Okot filled the tin pot and enameled mug with kernels, and dumped them in one of the saddlebags that was already emptied of dried venison.

That evening it was so cold they decided they had to risk making a fire. First they unrolled Paul's oilskin and stretched it out like a tent between two crooked spruce trees. Just then a burst of wind snatched it from their hands. It sailed up, up, up, and the wind whipped it around the high branches of one of the trees.

Chip went pale. He said, "This bad sign. We not sleep here tonight. Great Spirit be angry. We find new place."

Paul knew better by now than to try to argue with Chip when he was worried about his Great Spirit. "Let's go on then," he said.

So they packed up again. Okot shinnied up the tree and tugged at the oilskin until it was finally free. The wind was blowing fiercely by then and he had a hard time getting down with the bulky cloth. Chip rolled his eyes in fear. He kept saying, "Let go. Leave here. Great Spirit speak to us."

But Paul said, "We have to have it, Chip. It's the only thing we have that will keep the rain out."

It was getting dark. Tiredly they led the horses on. It turned out, though, to be a good move. After ten minutes of walking they came to a steep hill with many rocky outcroppings. About halfway up they found a deep, narrow cave, facing north. It was well sheltered, out of the wind, and scrub trees provided them with twigs and cones to make a fire. A fall of rocks blocked off part of the mouth of the cave. Chip said, "Aiee!" softly but happily when he saw this. They could build a fire inside the cave up against the rocks. That would reflect the heat back inside. And their fire was not likely to be seen by anyone who might be around.

Chip scouted around the ridge while Paul and Okot gathered tinder and brush. The pinecones were heavy with resin, and the twigs dry as bones. They soon had a small fire crackling away. "Cozy," Chip said when he joined them, and they laughed. They spread out the oilskin and the bedroll, and sat by the fire chewing on their dried venison while they talked about what was to come.

Chip said, "Three more days, maybe four, and I think we see my village. I think we near the place I crossed when we started hunt. Tomorrow we take this way." He pointed to the east.

"What will they think about us?" Paul asked for the hundredth time. "Will your clan be angry that you're with a white man?"

Chip said, "You are my friends. My people will welcome my friends. There have been no battles for a long time." He held out his arm with the wristband. "Blood brothers," he said firmly.

Paul put his on top of Chip's. "Friends forever," he said.

And then Okot put his wrist on Paul's. "No matter what happens."

They grinned at each other in the firelight. Whatever happened tomorrow, it would be all right, because they were together.

Chip yawned enormously and curled up to sleep. But Paul got up and slipped outside. Okot watched him. He knew Paul had gone to pray. After a minute he followed, and found Paul sitting with his back against a rock, staring off to the north. Okot sat beside him. "Paul," he said, "when you just talked to your Jesus God, what did you say?"

Paul shifted uncomfortably. "Well. Um. I—uh—I prayed for you and Chip to know God's love. I prayed for you to know the Lord Jesus as your Savior."

"You mean, for us to be Christians?"

"Yeah. And I asked God to help us be friends forever, and to help us and protect us. And I asked Him to help me find my father."

"All those things?" Okot said in wonder. "Don't He get tired of hearin' you?"

"Well, no. Never. The Bible says He always hears His children when they pray. And I'm one of His children."

"Paul, what's 'Lord' mean?"

"It means 'Master,'" Paul said. The moon was shining brightly enough for them to see, and he watched Okot's face. "Jesus is a good Master, Okot. Not like your Master Abbot, or Mister Payne. Jesus loves you."

Okot took a deep breath. "I think I want your Jesus God Lord Savior to be my Master. I want to see Him with my heart, like Mandy said. I don't want this bad feeling inside of me all the time. How do I talk to Him?"

"You can talk to Jesus right now. You can close your eyes if you want. I usually do, because then I don't think about other things. Then tell Him what you just told me. Tell Him you're sorry for all the bad things inside you, and thank Him for dying on the cross to take your punishment. Thank Him for forgiving you and being your Lord and Savior."

"Can I talk to Him in my own language? Cause it's better in my head than English. Does God understand Monyjang?"

Paul tried hard not to laugh. "Of course. You can talk to Him in any language. He understands everything."

Okot closed his eyes. He felt that strange warm feeling again, but he was afraid too. They were in the land of the Great Spirit. Would Chip's god be angry and make things go wrong? Or would the tribal spirits of the Dinka know that he was praying to a different God, and come to torment them?

Paul, watching Okot, wondered what struggles were going on inside the black boy's head and heart. Silently he prayed that the Holy Spirit would finish His work of opening Okot's heart to the truth.

After a few minutes Paul saw Okot's lips moving, but he couldn't understand the whispered words. He waited.

Okot decided to do what Paul said, and talk to God from his heart. "Dear Jesus God, I don't really know much about you. But Paul and Mandy are the kindest people I've ever known. If they love you, you must be the best Master and Friend there is. So, if it's all right, I would like to be your child too, 'cause I don't have a father or mother any more, and if you're who Paul and Mandy say you are, knowing you must be the best thing in the world. So please, Jesus, let me see you with my heart and be my Lord Jesus Savior God."

After a minute, Okot opened his eyes. Paul, sitting next to him, smiled. Okot felt suddenly shy. Paul said, "How do you feel?"

Feel? Okot didn't know. He rubbed his chest over his heart, but nothing seemed different. But all at once it seemed as though he could hear Mandy singing her song: "Swing low, sweet chariot, comin' for to carry me home...." He stood up and stared off into the darkness. "Where's home, Paul? I don't got no home."

"You do now, Okot. You have a home forever with Jesus. And you have a home with any Christians you meet. Including me. Remember, friends forever!"

Okot frowned. "But what about Chip?"

"We can both pray for him now."

They walked back to the cave. Chip was sitting up, carving a feather stick. He looked suspiciously from one to the other. "You be long time. And why this big smiles?"

"I have a new Master!" Okot burst out. "Jesus God has come into my heart."

"You mean you be Christian like white men now?"

"Not jus' white men is Christians," Okot said. "Jesus God is for every color of peoples."

Now what will Thunder Arm say? Chip wondered. But he felt a strange kind of emptiness inside, as though he hadn't eaten for a long time. As they stretched out around the fire to sleep, Chip lay with his deerskin wristband under his cheek to comfort himself. "Blood brothers," he whispered into the darkness.

Okot couldn't sleep for a long time. "My Master," he kept saying softly, to himself. And for the first time since the slave raiders came to Nyamlel he didn't feel alone.

Chip slept uneasily that night, disturbed by dreams of spirits battling in the heavens. He would have slept even worse if he knew that outside, a stone's throw downwind of the cave, a dark figure crouched behind an out-flung boulder. He had war paint on his face and body, and new feathers in his headdress. The light of the moon glinted faintly on the white bone arrowheads in his quiver.

Chapter 19

The Language of War

When they woke in the morning it looked as if the sky had fallen in. The fog was so thick they could hardly see the ground where they walked, and the horses drifted by like ghostly ships as they grazed in front of the cave. Okot's thin body shook with cold.

Chip slipped off into the gray murk. But he was back in seconds, running as fast as he could with his twisted leg swinging out at every step. "Someone was here," he hissed, holding out a feather. "Is war feather. From Haudenosaunee scout. This French trapper, him was right. Is braves on warpath. We must go."

Paul and Okot felt like blind men as they set off. Enemy scouts could be all around them and they wouldn't know it. What other dangers lurked just beyond the thick curtain of fog? Every muffled noise made their hearts jerk painfully. Was that the sound of a footfall in the dank leaves beside the trail? Or only a pinecone falling to the ground? Once a fox burst from a mist-shrouded copse and ran across their path, causing Storm to snort and shy.

Okot, riding behind Paul, clamped his hands firmly on the back of Storm's saddle. He could feel Paul's rigid back in front of him. *Is he afraid too?* Okot wondered. "Is it any good prayin' to God now?" he whispered.

"What d'you think I'm doing?" Paul whispered back. Chip twisted around to look at them, and put a warning finger to his lips, so they went on in silence.

Chip was having his own troubles. Proudfoot was restive, tossing his head and jumping at every whisper in the grass, threatening to bolt at the slightest opportunity. Chip's bad leg was cramped and throbbing in the cold damp air. Between that and Proudfoot's skittishness, he was forced to sling his bow over his shoulder so that he could hold his horse tightly reined in.

A sudden burst of clamoring blue jays made Proudfoot rear and bolt. Chip hung on grimly. *Danger!* he thought, fighting to stop his panicked horse. *Something is hiding in this fog. Or someone.*

The silence after the chattering of the jays was even harder to take. And now he couldn't see Paul or Okot. He couldn't call them either, without warning a concealed enemy.

Stealthily, Chip reached into the pouch at his waist and pulled out his dried rattle. He shook it once, twice, three times, and strained his ears to listen. Yes! There it was—an answering rattle. *That was Okot's,* Chip thought. In a moment he heard Paul's. Nudging Proudfoot sideways, he found his way back to his friends.

They moved on. The soft thudding of the horses' hooves sounded like the distant booming of guns, their breathing harsh and unnatural in the eerie stillness. Their hands grew sticky on the reins.

And then Chip heard it. The trilling of a chickadee, followed swiftly by the broken cry of a killdeer. But those birds would not sing in the fog. *Signals,* Chip thought. *Like the kind used by my people.* He strained his ears, and from behind heard the liquid seesawing whistles of a robin. The hairs prickled on the back of his head.

A cold wind sprang up from the north and began to blow away the fog. Ahead of them Chip saw the morning sun glow weakly over the treetops. It was an angry red like a great scabby wound in the sky. Chip shuddered. *The Great Spirit is angry,* he thought.

The birdcalls came again, the killdeer and the robin. And then Chip's heart thudded painfully. "Twee-twee-toyou-toyou-chack-chack-wheep-wheep." He heard the familiar disjointed couplets of a thrasher, the bird the color of horse chestnuts that always perched high in the trees to sing, its head thrown back like a proud warrior brave.

But this was not a real thrasher. The call came from directly ahead of them, on the open trail. Before Chip could warn Paul and Okot, an icy blast of wind tore away the drifting mist. A brave on horseback stood squarely on the trail, not ten paces away.

Chip twisted around. Behind them a second warrior blocked the way they had come. Storm snorted and pawed restlessly at the turf. Paul and Okot looked to the left, and then to the right. They were surrounded!

For a long moment time stood still. Even the wind seemed to stop blowing. The warriors and their horses were like carved stone figures; only the feathers stirred in their headbands. *This is it,* Paul thought. *Now we're going to die in an Indian attack after all.* Okot's hope that these warriors were Chip's people was dashed by one glance at Chip's tense face.

And then they charged. It happened so fast, without any kind of signal seeming to pass from one to the other, that Chip had no chance to get an arrow on his bowstring.

But I couldn't shoot them anyway, he thought wildly, trying to keep Proudfoot under control. *These are my Haudenosaunee.*

Storm kicked and bucked as the warriors rushed in on them. Then he pulled back, rearing and thrashing the air with his hooves as one of the braves grabbed hold of his bridle. Okot was thrown violently into the air. The moment he hit the ground he was swept up roughly by one of the warriors. "No! No!" he shrieked in his own language. "Let me go!" All his terror of being captured again came sweeping over him, wiping out any fear of what these Indians might do to him. "No one's gonna chain me up again!" he shouted in English. But all his struggling was useless. The warrior's grip was like the crushing bite of a crocodile. He manhandled Okot back onto Storm behind Paul.

Almost before they knew it was happening the two of them had been lashed together with strong buckskin thongs. Their arms were tied to their sides, and the bindings cut into their skin through their ragged shirts. It was a terrible feeling, being so helpless. But worse was the silence of the stony-faced braves.

Meanwhile, they saw that Chip's bow and quiver of arrows had been taken away from him, along with his knife. But now one of the warriors was looking carefully at the bow, and he said something tersely to the others. Chip broke in excitedly, pouring out words in his Onondaga language, pointing to the bow and to the carving on the handle of his knife.

The braves glanced up, again and again, at Okot, and Paul was sure their eyes rolled with fear. Probably they'd never seen a black man. Finally, with a last brief exchange of words, they set off at a brisk trot. Two of the braves led

Storm and Proudfoot by the reins. Chip was not tied up, and when he was alongside Paul and Okot he said in a low voice, "These braves is Onondaga. Their chief is Eagle Wing. Sister of my father is wife of him. These braves riding to Ohsweken. Is big war party there. We go to their camp. They not trust me now, but will when Eagle Wing see me."

"You mean they don't trust you because of us," Paul said.

Reluctantly Chip nodded. "Them don't ever trust white men. They go now to make war on white settlers. And them mighty scared of Okot," he added. "Them think him's an evil spirit come to bring trouble. Them say Great Spirit angry."

At that moment the last of the fog blew away from the treetops and the sun blazed down bright and yellow in the frosty blue sky. Chip spoke in Onondaga to the brave who was leading Proudfoot. "You see. The Great Spirit is not angry. These are my friends. Their color doesn't matter. They are friends of the Onondaga."

The warrior just grunted. They rode the rest of the way in silence.

The war party was camped in a wide cornfield—about fifty braves with their horses. *But there must be more out patrolling the area,* Chip thought. *Like the ones who caught us.* Paul and Okot were taken off Storm and tied up separately. A brave took away Paul's knife, but he didn't search them so Okot's knife stayed safely hidden under his loose shirt. Chip was taken away to speak with Eagle Wing, but a brave was left to guard Paul and Okot, so they couldn't talk to each other about what was happening.

They were hungry and thirsty, and terribly sore from being tied up, by the time Chip came back. Chip was worried about his friends, but still excited at being back with his people again. "I sorry Eagle Wing say you must be tied up," he said, sitting cross-legged beside them. "Him ask me many questions. I tell him you my friends. We like brothers. Him not happy. Onondaga are riding to war. First we go to Ohsweken. That is two days' riding away, but Eagle Wing say is big hurry, so we ride hard and come there tonight. Then to war by River of Thunder. Niagara."

"War with who?" Paul wanted to know.

"War with white settlers," Chip said miserably. "Onondaga angry that white men build new village. New house for white God. This very bad, but there is more bad. Some white man has killed an Onondaga brave of our Hotahyonhne clan. One moon ago. Eagle Wing and Thunder Arm make war council with other chiefs in Ohsweken."

At last Okot and Paul were untied, but two braves kept arrows pointed at them while they ate a meal of pemmican and bannock. It was so still that a chickadee landed between Okot's outstretched legs, and he threw it a few crumbs. In a moment another one fluttered down, hopping onto the chunk of bannock he was holding. He tore off a piece and, just as he was about to eat it, the bird snatched it from his hand. Okot stared open-mouthed and Paul burst out laughing. "Now that's a real brave for you!" he said. "The settlers say it's a good sign when a flighty bird like a chickadee comes close like that."

"Some sign," Okot muttered as the first chickadee flitted up to his hand and pecked at his bannock. "It's a sign that I's gonna stay hungry." But the cheeky little black-capped birds cheered him up, at least until they set off again along the trail.

Paul and Okot weren't tied up again to ride, but they were herded into the middle of the war party and closely watched by the warriors surrounding them. Okot tried to concentrate on the long snaking column of riders in front of them, and Chip riding at the head of the line with Eagle Wing. But he felt the black eyes of the braves boring into him.

Paul simply felt the terrible weight of their hatred for all white men. *Has Chip deserted us, now that he's back among his own people?* he wondered. But all at once he and Okot saw Chip raise his arm with the braided wristband and wave it in the air. "We're still blood brothers," Paul whispered in Okot's ear, and they both felt better.

All day and all evening, until the waning moon had risen high in the cold dark sky, they kept on at a steady lope, slowing to a walk only when the tough Indian horses began to falter. Flecks of foam flew from their mouths and landed on their heaving chests and in their riders' faces. Chip's twisted leg hung nearly useless down Proudfoot's side, and he only stayed upright by instinct. Okot felt a strange burning along the insides of his thighs, and his hands were raw from gripping the reins. Only Paul was still relaxed and fresh on Storm. He was used to such long days in the saddle when he traveled with his father. He never wanted the ride to end—but not because he was enjoying himself. He just wanted to put off facing whatever was happening at Ohsweken.

At long last a ripple of excitement ran through the party. Eagle Wing slowed everyone to a walk. A scout had gone ahead to Ohsweken, and so Thunder Arm was waiting for them with a small band of warriors outside the village palisade. Chip let out a whoop of joy and kicked the exhausted Proudfoot into a run again. They pounded over the hard-packed earth up to his father.

Thunder Arm reached out and touched Chip's shoulder with affection. "The Great Spirit has brought back my son. And you bear the scars of a warrior brave. I am pleased."

They rode on into Ohsweken. The village was dark and silent, but a few of the braves carried burning torches—including Chip's brother Swift Deer, who came forward to grasp him by the leg. They all looked with awe at the terrible scars on Proudfoot's flank, at the great purple scar on Chip's face and his twisted leg. Okot they gave sidelong, suspicious glances. He shivered and held on tighter to Paul's waist as Storm snorted and sidled away. He could feel the white boy shivering through his thin shirt. But then the braves were touching Paul's wolf pelt and jabbering about it, grinning and pointing at him with approving nods. Paul began to feel better. One of them took hold of Storm's bridle and fondled the big albino's head until he began to calm down.

"Where's Black Hawk?" Chip wanted to know, scanning the group in the dusk. But Thunder Arm and Eagle Wing were already summoning the braves to the war council around the central fire in the longhouse, and Chip got no answer. Swift Deer helped him slide off Proudfoot, and Chip staggered as his twisted leg hit the ground. Paul and Okot dismounted stiffly, and they were herded with Chip to a room near the end of the main passage. "Is beside my family room," Chip told them, but there was nothing in it but a heap of thick black bearskin rugs.

A young girl brought them bannock, roast squash and venison to eat. Okot felt his heart skip a beat when he looked into her face. She had soft, doe-like brown eyes just like Mandy's. Chip jumped up and hugged her. "Dawn on Water!" he cried, in his own language. "I am happy to see you." He turned to Okot and Paul. "Is my sister," he explained.

The girl smiled shyly, but she couldn't help staring wide-eyed at Okot and Paul. She had never been this close to a white man, and had never seen a black person at all. She disappeared, but returned soon with an armful of buckskin clothing. She and Chip exchanged a few words, and then she left them alone again.

"Is for all of us," Chip explained through a mouthful of bannock. "Thunder Arm calls for me to speak to war council. We must go now."

They sorted through the shirts and leggings, finding the biggest for Paul, and the smallest for Chip. Okot's were too wide and short again for his long thin body, but the buckskin was soft as a spring rain on his skin. He and Paul looked at each other and both said, "Aiee!" at the same time.

"You make good braves," Chip said. "Dawn on Water has made these clothes. And the beads are her work." Their shirts were beaded with intricate designs that gleamed like liquid silver and turquoise in the torchlight. "Now we go. You not speak to war council. After, I tell you what is said."

Chip led the way boldly to the meeting place, but inside he was quaking. He had never seen his father so grim, so stern and austere in his greeting. Paul and Okot could feel the thick tension in the air, but they were so amazed with their new clothes and their surroundings that they forgot about being scared.

Thunder Arm's questions for Chip were brief. "Who are these strangers you call friends? What tribe is the black one from?"

Chip answered in their Onondaga language. "He comes from another land over the great salt lake. It is many moons' journey from here." Then Chip told his father about Paul. Thunder Arm nodded. He had met the Reverend Brentwood at the trading post. But this did not make him happy that Paul was traveling with his son. "You call this white boy your friend. Do you call his God your friend too?"

"No, Father. I am Onondaga."

"You understand that we must make war. These people are not part of our plans. But they must come now. To send them back to a white man's settlement means that others will hear what we are planning. The Redcoats will arrive before our war party and warn the people away. We will be attacked with guns, and many will die. They may die. Do you understand?"

Chip licked his dry lips. "But Father, why must they all die? If you told the white men's army there has been murder, then they would find the person who did it."

"That would not give us our land back. Or get rid of their God from the land of the Great Spirit. Eagle Wing tells me you have said this Paul and Okot are like brothers to you. But I tell you this, my son. Your own brother, Black Hawk, has been murdered. The firstborn of your mother's body is dead. For this the white men will pay with their blood."

Chip felt the room spin crazily around him. He swayed and almost fell. Instinctively Paul and Okot grabbed his arms and held him. They thought it was just because Chip's bad leg was giving out after the hours and hours of hard riding. But when they looked at the grim faces of the war council, and at the cold sweat on Chip's forehead, they knew something terrible was wrong.

Thunder Arm spoke again. His words were harsh and explosive. The other elders beat the ground in front of them. It seemed to Chip that his heart was being battered like an anvil with a blacksmith's hammer. He could scarcely breathe. But he had enough sense left in him to be glad that the friendship wristbands that he and the others wore were hidden under their new buckskin shirts. Now would not be a good time for Thunder Arm to be questioning him about the pact he had made with his friends.

Abruptly Thunder Arm raised his arm in dismissal. In a daze, Chip turned away and stumbled down the passage. Paul and Okot followed him back to their room.

It was a few minutes before Chip could speak. He felt hot and cold at the same time. He had a long drink of water from the skin hanging on the wall, but then he thought he was going to vomit. Paul and Okot watched him anxiously. "Oh, is terrible thing," Chip whispered finally, as they all curled up in the bearskin rugs. "It is my brother, my brother Black Hawk, who has been killed."

Okot and Paul listened, horrified, as Chip struggled to talk. "This be a knife in heart of Thunder Arm. This village we go to burn. These people we go to kill. It is in Thunder Arm's heart that no one must live, because a white man has killed so great an Onondaga warrior, his son, his firstborn son who should be chief. We ride tomorrow, and the next day is war. A surprise attack, before the sun come up."

"We have to leave here," Paul whispered, sitting up. "Leave and get to Middleport. There's a militia regiment there. Redcoats. We can warn them. They'll be able to beat the war party. Save the town, and the people. And find out who killed your brother."

"But you not leave," Chip said unhappily. "Is guards over doors now. Thunder Arm not want any word out. Oh, Paul." Chip turned his miserable gaze on his friend. "Thunder Arm has told me. Your father is alive. Not hurt by Indians when war party ambush you two moons ago. But now he helps build the new God-house at Niagara. And this party—these my clan warriors—is sworn to kill him first."

Chapter 20

Thunder in the Distance

Before dawn Paul and Okot were woken up by the sound of drums. They heard chanting, and strange yips like the sound of many dogs. The ground shook with the stamping of feet.

An eerie flickering light danced on the walls of their room. They shook off their warm bearskin rugs and stood shivering in the nippy air, stretching and yawning. Chip was gone—in fact, the whole longhouse seemed to be deserted.

They walked out to the main entrance and stopped dead in their tracks.

Dozens of warriors were dancing to the throbbing of the drums. They went in a circle around a center post, whooping and leaping in the air. Their faces were painted, and they had black charcoal markings on their arms and legs. They carried lances, bows and tomahawks, and quivers of arrows on their shoulders. Sweat shone on their limbs and brows, and they stabbed in a frenzy at the post with their tomahawks and lances.

Chip stood just outside the circle, by a huge campfire. He was holding a tomahawk and watching it all with his black eyes sparkling. Paul remembered the things they had talked about through the night and his stomach churned with betrayal. He thought about his friend

Freeman, who must have faced a band of warriors like this before he was killed in the Indian massacre, and the blood froze in his veins.

An hour passed, or more. Then suddenly the drumbeat changed. The warriors gave one last wild yelp. Then there was silence.

Paul and Okot had no chance to talk to Chip before they and all the braves—about a hundred of them, from Ohsweken and other villages around the area—were mounted and ready to leave for Niagara. The warriors had arrived in small bands over the last two weeks so that they wouldn't attract attention from the white settlements. Now, Thunder Arm and Eagle Wing dispatched them to Niagara in the same small bands. Each was told how to approach the newly cleared land where the settlers were building, and where to hide in the woods until the order came to attack. "Go swift and silent as wolves in the winter snows," Thunder Arm said, and then the palisade gates were opened.

Chip, Paul and Okot rode in a small party led by Swift Deer. Okot had been given a horse of his own, a tall pinto suited to his long legs. The gelding, called Raveneye, was fresh and strong, and Okot struggled to control him. *All I need right now is to fall off,* he thought frantically. He'd be embarrassed to death if he didn't get trampled to death first.

They'd only been riding a few minutes before they had to ford a river. The horses, crazed with excitement, plunged eagerly down the banks and into the fast-flowing icy water. Okot clung to Raveneye's neck, and tried to keep his skinny legs wrapped around the horse's belly when he began to swim in the deep water. The motion was as strange as it had been on the slave ship, but nicer, and after a minute Okot relaxed.

Too soon. Suddenly Raveneye and the other horses were scrambling up the far bank, heaving themselves over the slippery stones and muddy soil. Raveneye pulled free of the sucking mud with a great bucking leap. Okot felt himself flying high into the air. He held on desperately to the horse's mane, and for a moment he hung upside down, staring at the ground flashing past below him. Then, with a great thump he landed on his belly, half on and half off Raveneye's back. The horse lunged forward again, and Okot regained his seat, panting and gasping for air. Raveneye turned his head and gave Okot a baleful stare. "Oh, turn around and run," Okot muttered, clutching the reins with one hand and rubbing his bruised stomach with the other. "I's gonna do better next time."

Paul cantered up beside him on Storm. He had watched with horror as Okot nearly came off Raveneye in the path of the stampeding horses. But then he had laughed, and he was still trying to keep a straight face. "Hey, Philip Astley!" he shouted. "You thinking of starting a new circus in Upper Canada?"

Philip Astley? Circus? Okot shook his head, frowning, and Paul laughed out loud. "I'll tell you later," he called into the wind, and it whipped his words away like smoke from a chimney.

Chip had been riding up front, trying to speak to his brother. But Swift Deer's face was set into hard lines, and he only spoke once, sharply. "We ride to war, Chipagawana. But you are only a boy, and not a brave. Stay back, and keep silent." Hurt and confused, Chip dropped back in the group to ride between Paul and Okot.

It was impossible to talk until they slowed down to wind their way through a grove of scrub oak and ash saplings. By then, all laughter had left Okot and Paul, and Chip noticed their troubled faces. *They can't be scared,* he thought. *Paul's always saying how he trusts his God, and now Okot says he trusts Him too. So why do they look so miserable?*

Okot finally broke the silence. "Chip, did you change your mind about what we's talked about last night? About the fightin' tomorrow?"

"No!" he shouted.

"So we still do what we planned?" Paul asked, looking sideways at his friend. "Because you looked different this morning." *Like a brave on the warpath,* he wanted to add, but he bit his tongue and didn't say it out loud.

Chip suddenly realized how the war dance must have looked to them. And they were right. It *was* a terrible sight. It sent shivers down his back just thinking about it, remembering the chanting and thudding of moccasined feet on the packed earth. Excitement made his blood run hot again. But he shook his head at his friends. "I am Onondaga," he said. "That never change. I got to feel this good here—" he thumped his chest "—when I see my clan braves do this dance. But you are my blood brothers. Thunder Arm *not* spill blood of my brother Paul's father."

Okot and Paul breathed deep sighs of relief. But Okot suddenly realized what had been niggling at him ever since they set out. "Chip, where's your bow and arrows?"

Chip hissed like a trapped wildcat. "Thunder Arm not let me have these back. Him not trust me because of my friends. Him say I betray Hotahyonhne clan with arrows."

"We're sorry," Paul said.

But Chip grinned at him. "Is okay. Thunder Arm right."

There was no time to say more. They came out of the trees and Swift Deer raised his arm high. The horses broke into a jog again, and they settled into another grueling run.

They crossed countless rivers and streams during the day, stopping only to allow the horses to drink. Sometimes, in the distance, Okot saw plumes of smoke rising from the chimneys of white settlements, and wondered what kind of a life he was going to find when the battle was over. The pounding of Raveneye's hooves under him seemed to beat out a rhythm that echoed the pounding in his head. *If only I had some kind of a home.... If only I knew someone who helps runaway slaves.... If only...*

Now they went more slowly, as the settlements crowded closer to their path and the sun dipped lower in the sky. They glided noiselessly along the edges of ploughed fields and dark woods. Okot began to hear a faint booming, like far-off gunfire. He raised his chin from where it had sunk wearily onto his chest. "What's that?" he whispered to Chip.

"Niagara," Chip told him excitedly. "Soon we see mighty River of Thunder." His eyes shone. "Is my first time to see this big waterfalls." Then he ducked his head, ashamed. "I wish it was with hunting party, not with war party."

Soon the sound of roaring water filled the air, even though all around them were the same wooded glades. Then they burst out from the forest's edge, and there was the river, crashing over rocks deep in a gorge below them.

Here they stopped to rest while Swift Deer consulted with the older braves. Chip, Paul and Okot huddled together on the rough grassy ground, forcing down more of the wearisome pemmican. "Trout would be good right now," Paul said, to relieve the tension.

"Milking time," Okot said dreamily. "A big gourd full of fresh milk's what I want."

"What will happen to you, Chip?" Paul asked. "After what we're going to do, will Thunder Arm ever forgive you?"

Chip's face was dark with anger and gloom. The scar on his forehead and cheek stood out against his dusky skin like a white birch branch against the night sky. "I not think about this," he said finally. "But we must find man who kill Black Hawk."

The thin crescent of a new moon was high in the sky when they finally came to the end of their ride. They'd had just a quick glimpse of the falls, and now they were hidden in thick woods near the edge of the new white settlement. There was nothing to do but wait—for the morning, and the battle.

Thunder Arm had appeared only minutes after their band settled in for the night, and Chip was summoned to talk with him and Swift Deer. Paul was sunk in the deepest misery he had ever known. Somewhere out there, just beyond the edge of the trees, was his father. And he might never see him again, except dead with Thunder Arm's arrows through his heart. Okot sat with his friend, leaning against the trunk of a huge old maple tree, but he didn't know what to say. He was remembering what it was like to see his own father lying dead with a spear in his side.

Facing Thunder Arm was the hardest thing Chip had ever done, because he knew his father would be able to read his eyes. Would he guess that Chip was planning to betray him to the white men?

Thunder Arm's first words came as a relief. "Chipagawana, a dark spirit has visited me this night," he said. "I saw you in battle with the white men, with arrows all around. But you are not yet a brave, even though you have fought with a bear and a wolf. You will not ride with us in the morning."

"But Father, you have seen that I have the scars of fighting, just like a brave. I have fought a wolverine too, and killed a buck. You said yourself that I would save my people from danger."

"Someday you will. I still believe that. But not tomorrow. You and the other two will stay here, or you will be outcast from Ohsweken, and from the longhouse of your mother."

Paul and Okot were both relieved when Chip reappeared at last through the trees. But he was followed by his father and brother. Chip spoke to his friends quickly, stumbling over his words and looking worriedly between them and Thunder Arm. "Thunder Arm say he tie you up. Him say you be big danger to war party. Him not trust no white man. And him afraid of Okot. Him say is bad sign from spirits." Thunder Arm broke in, his voice fierce even though he was speaking in a whisper. Chip listened, and then he translated, "My father say, if you make vow to your God not to join side with Brentwood, him not make you tied up."

"You mean I should just sit here while they massacre my people?" Paul said to Chip. He was whispering, but his fists were clenched tight.

"You must say yes," Chip hissed urgently. "Or him tie all of us up, and we not be able to do what we plan."

But if I make this vow, Paul thought, *I can't break it. My father would rather die than let me break a promise to God.* He shut his eyes tight for a second, and prayed fiercely under his breath, "Dear Jesus, please work this out." Then he looked straight at Thunder Arm. "All right," he said. "I promise."

Chip spoke to his father. Thunder Arm nodded gravely. Swift Deer hadn't said a word. They glided off into the woods, and the boys were alone again.

"Now what?" Paul muttered.

"Is something strange with Swift Deer," Chip said, sitting cross-legged in front of them. "Him not say any words to me. Not speak to Thunder Arm."

"I guess he must be awfully sad about Black Hawk being killed," Paul said. "But what are we going to do?"

"We go," Chip said.

"But I promised," Paul said miserably.

"Promised not to join the settlers' side," Okot pointed out. "We can still do what we said, to stop the killin'. Just that we got to do it all alone."

"So," Chip said, "this is what we must do." And he whispered to them while the woods sank into deeper darkness.

The night seemed endless. Once their plans were ready they huddled together for warmth under Paul's bedroll and tried to sleep. But Chip lay awake and troubled. Whatever happened in the morning, nothing in his life would be the same again.

At last the new moon set behind the trees and there was a faint stirring in the woods as the braves mounted their horses. Then, like the ghost of a breeze coming with the sunrise, Swift Deer glided through the trees to stand over Chip. A daring robin, just starting its dawn song, faltered and fell silent.

"My brother the brave!" Swift Deer muttered scornfully. "Sleeping like a little girl while the men go to war." He spat on the ground, then twisted on his heels and was gone.

Chip, pretending to be asleep, cringed with shame under the bedroll. He wished he could shout back at his brother, "I'm going to show you! I'm as much a brave as you are!" But he had to lie silent with his eyes closed until he was sure that Swift Deer and the others were well out of sight, on their way to the freshly cleared land where the white settlers slept.

Only then he roused Paul and Okot. They woke silently and quickly to the pressure of Chip's fingers behind their left ears. They got up stiffly, yawning with tiredness and nerves. They could see their breath in the icy morning air, and they had to stamp their feet to get the circulation going. Chip led them to where the horses were squealing with indignation at being left behind, and straining against their tethers.

Okot's muscles screamed in protest when he tried to mount Raveneye. It took him three tries, and finally he had to pull himself up with the help of an overhanging branch. Raveneye gave him another spiteful look, and Chip laughed. "Him wonder what kind of brave you be," he said. But he couldn't make his twisted leg behave either, and had to let Paul give him a leg up onto Proudfoot. "Him mighty sore brave," Okot said. "Just like Chipawagana."

"Chipawagana?" Chip spluttered. "Ugh! Better you should still say Chip."

Okot was miffed. He had been practicing, because he wanted to please Chip. "I thought that was right."

"Chip-a-GA-WAN-a!" Chip said. But then he grinned. "Thanks you for trying."

Paul jumped easily into Storm's saddle. Chip and Okot rolled their eyes at each other, and they both muttered, "Showoff!" But their hearts pounded in their throats as the laughter left Chip's face. He wheeled Proudfoot around and set off in the opposite direction to the one taken by the war party. He rode fast through the formless darkness, a blurry movement ahead of Paul and Okot. They brushed past bare twigs and sharp spruce branches without feeling them.

Even now, they knew, the bands of warriors were taking up their positions around the settlement. In the shadowed edges of the trees they would encircle the newly cleared area so that, when Thunder Arm and Eagle Wing gave the signal to attack, the settlers wouldn't have any chance of escape. "When braves attack," Chip had told them, "if white men go in houses, then braves set them on fire."

Paul and Okot were horrified. Chip shrugged. "Is warrior way. But we stop Thunder Arm before this."

"Maybe the Redcoats will come," Paul had said wistfully. But Chip shook his head. "Eagle Wing say Redcoats is two days' riding away. That be why we attack now. And this new moon. Much dark."

The thunderous roar from Niagara Falls was all around them now, the air damp with mist in the pearly light of dawn. Only a thin line of bushes hid them from sight of the settlement camp. Okot strained his ears to hear another sound—the stamping of a hoof, a cough or a sneeze. There was nothing. Next to Niagara, the silence was like a heavy weight on his soul. He hardly dared breathe.

Chip reined in Proudfoot and faced his friends. "Very soon it be time," he whispered solemnly. "Is most danger for you. When braves fight—maybe nothing stop them. Will be many arrows…"

"Any of us might be killed," Paul said softly. "Chip, you and Okot should stay here. Only I have to do this. They are my people."

"You said they's Christians," Okot whispered. "That makes'em my people now too, don't it?"

"Anyway, we your brothers," Chip reminded him. "We is sworn. We go."

Over the noise of the falls they heard, suddenly, the kee-wick kee-wick of an owl. "Twee-twee-toyou-toyou-chack-chack-wheep-wheep," came the immediate reply, and Paul and Okot felt goose bumps on their arms. It was the call of a thrasher—the same one they had heard just before they were captured by Eagle Wing's scouts. Chip's face hardened with tension, and they knew it was his people signaling each other.

Chip held out his arm and rolled up the sleeve of his buckskin shirt so that his wristband showed. Paul and Okot did the same, and they crossed their wrists. "If one of us gets killed, then we won't be no threefold cord no more," Okot said suddenly.

"You'll always have God," Paul said. "My father always said—says—that one man with God on his side is stronger than anyone else."

For a second, Chip looked as though he had just eaten a hunk of rotten raccoon. Paul could have bitten off his tongue. But then Chip grunted. "Is Him strong enough to stop arrows?"

"Well—sure. He has done."

"Good. Then we not killed. We stay threefold friends."

At that second a strident yip-yip-yipping pierced the air. The attack had begun!

Chapter 21

New Beginnings

The sound of the warriors swelled and grew into a crazed howling that made Paul's heart stop. But he had no time to think. "Now!" Chip cried, gouging Proudfoot's sides cruelly with his heels. "Fast, fast, fast!" he yelled over his shoulder. Storm and Raveneye needed no urging. They flew after Proudfoot, bursting from cover and sweeping across the clearing. And then they were storming into the path of the shrieking warriors!

For a second—a fraction of a second—Paul had a glimpse of the clearing. He saw the smoke curling up from a dozen campfires. He saw makeshift lean-tos covered with oilskins, rough board tables and tin coffeepots and lumpy shapes of bedrolls. He saw the rectangles of the half-finished log buildings…everything shining ghostly silver as the rising sun lighted the misty air. It was so still, so peaceful, that it could have been a painting. And in the middle of it all, standing in breeches and a homespun shirt with his arms raised to heaven, was Paul's father.

That picture would be frozen in Paul's memory forever—but the moment was swept from him as he and Storm met the raging mass of frenzied warriors. The air was thick with flying arrows and dust. Something zinged past Paul's head and he felt feathers brush his cheek. Then he saw Eagle Wing, and kicked Storm after the chief. Eagle

Wing had an arrow on the string and was taking aim at Brentwood!

"No!" Paul shrieked, driving Storm right into Eagle Wing's horse. Storm shied and reared up. Paul threw himself at the chief, lunging for his bow arm, and then he was falling…falling…but still clinging grimly to Eagle Wing. He heard the hideous scream of a horse, and saw Storm stumble to his knees with an arrow in his chest. "Oh, Storm, no!" he sobbed. But there was no time for tears. Eagle Wing was struggling with him, and all around them horses pounded by, leaping to clear the two wrestling figures on the trampled earth.

Okot had been the first to spy Swift Deer, galloping like a wild fiend from the other side of the circle. He hauled Raveneye around, kicking and lashing the pinto brutally to make him turn and thunder across the center of the camp. The horse lunged and bucked his way over two campfires, spattering settlers with burning embers. Why aren't they shooting the Indians? Okot wondered fleetingly, looking back over his shoulder. But he had no more time to think. He felt Raveneye hesitate and bunch his haunches underneath him. "Oh, no you don't!" he shouted, thinking the horse was going to buck again, and he smacked him with the ends of his reins. But when he turned, he saw a great pile of logs directly in their path. Before he could pull Raveneye away, the horse had leapt, nearly pulling Okot's arms out of their sockets as he tried to hang on. *We'll never make it,* he thought desperately, screwing his eyes shut. But in a moment they were over and pounding past the last building.

Swift Deer saw him coming. There was no hesitation in him. Without checking his horse's stride, he nocked an arrow and loosed it straight at Okot.

Not for nothing was Raveneye a warrior's horse. He didn't need Okot's heels to urge him out of the way. Okot heard the thud as the bone arrowhead bit into one of the logs behind him. The other warriors were streaming by, and arrow after arrow zipped past Okot, but he turned Raveneye's head back toward Swift Deer. *He really means to kill me,* he thought.

Suddenly a ferocious howling reached them from across the camp. Swift Deer reined his horse away from Okot's path and galloped off, yelling madly. Raveneye fishtailed around and was off after Swift Deer before Okot could react. He clutched a handful of mane and tried to stay on.

Earlier, Chip had seen Paul and Storm go down but he couldn't stop to help. He could see Thunder Arm at the head of the swarming braves, his headdress thick with war feathers blown nearly flat on his head by the speed of his galloping horse. Thunder Arm's bow was fully drawn and he was intent on one thing only—the figure of Brentwood, who was shepherding women and children into one of the unfinished buildings.

Thunder Arm was a terrifying figure on his great black stallion, and for a moment Chip quailed at the murderous rage in his father's eyes. But then, behind him, he heard Paul's sobbing shout. "*Stop him*, Chip! He's going to kill my *father*!"

Chip lashed Proudfoot on, straight toward the great barrel chest of Thunder Arm's horse. It towered above them, and now Thunder Arm saw his son. Chip was right in the line of fire. An arrow whistled past his head. And another. There was a cry of pain as someone behind him was hit.

At the shout from Paul, Brentwood had turned back to face the battle, and now he too saw Chip, and his own son tottering across the flattened grass. "Paul?" he cried, running to meet him. "Paul, my son!"

"No!" Paul yelled. "Go back! Get back!"

Zing! Thunder Arm loosed an arrow just as Proudfoot crashed head-on into his stallion. A cry went up as Brentwood reeled and fell. Blood spurted from his thigh.

Chip stood his ground. He held Proudfoot tightly reined in, trying to block Thunder Arm's sight on Brentwood. Thunder Arm raised his arm, stopping the attack. The warriors fought with their excited horses, circling about in confusion.

Twang! Another arrow came from behind. It was Swift Deer who had struck, shooting his arrow before Okot could stop him. With a barbaric howl Okot stood on Raveneye's back and flung himself onto Swift Deer, knocking them both to the ground. His face smacked the earth and he tasted blood. Then he and Swift Deer were locked together, wrestling. For a second Okot remembered wrestling with Paul in their clearing in the rain. It all seemed so long ago—another life—and now he was wrestling for his life. The blood sang in his ears and his mouth was full of blood and grit…then strong hands pulled him away, and he saw that several of the white men had taken hold of Swift Deer.

Okot staggered to his feet and turned around. Brentwood was on his side, with a great spreading stain on his chest. Paul was clutching his father and crying, "No! God, please, no!" But Brentwood's eyes were closed. He hardly seemed to be breathing.

Chip had slid off Proudfoot and was holding Thunder Arm's horse by the reins. The stallion reared, dragging

Chip off his feet and shaking him like a cat shaking a mouse. All the time Chip was pleading in Onondaga at his father. Thunder Arm, stony faced, sat like a statue on his mad horse. All around the air was full of choking dust and the smell of blood and sweating horses.

"Look out!" someone shouted.

Paul looked up and cried, "Eagle Wing! No!" The chief was on his knees, his bow fully drawn. But at the moment he released the arrow a figure broke from the group of settlers and flung himself across Brentwood. Already others were grabbing Eagle Wing and pinning his arms behind his back.

There was a thud, and a groan, and the man rolled off Brentwood. Paul looked at his face, and gasped. "Giant John!" he breathed.

The trapper had taken the arrow in his left shoulder. He was grimacing with pain, but he managed a mangled sort of grin. "Hey, Preacher," he groaned. "Is that gonna earn me any points with God?"

Brentwood's face was gray and glistened with sweat. His breathing was harsh and heavy. But his eyes opened and he said through gritted teeth, "We'll talk about you and God some other time. But thanks, John."

"Father?" Paul said. "Are you all right?"

And then he saw that the blood on Brentwood's chest was from an arrow stuck in his forearm, not in his heart. But the one in the trapper's shoulder would have finished him, because Eagle Wing had clearly been aiming for his neck. "Now that you're back, Paul, I'm all right," he said weakly. "Help me get up."

Giant John and Paul helped Brentwood to stand. At that moment Thunder Arm uttered a loud cry in Onondaga, with his arm held high. It sounded like a command.

Chip, pale faced, dropped the reins and stood before his father. The circling braves drew their horses to a halt. In moments the camp was still. The silence was eerie after all the shouting and confusion. Even the roaring of Niagara seemed to be hushed. Okot and Paul glanced at each other and licked their lips nervously. They were relieved when the wailing of a baby splintered the silence.

Brentwood walked up to Thunder Arm, leaning heavily on Paul and John. Blood oozed from his arm and thigh, and from John's shoulder, dropping and mingling on the dusty earth. Stopping beside Chip, Brentwood raised his good arm in the sign of peace. "Greetings, Chief Thunder Arm," he said, in the Indian's language. "Our people have a peace treaty with your clan. Why have you come unprovoked with your war party to do murder here?"

With great dignity, Thunder Arm dismounted. A brave led his horse away. The chief stood before Brentwood with his arms crossed in front of him. He ignored Chip completely. "We come for lawful blood," he said. "One of your settlers has killed an Onondaga brave. The Great Spirit is angry. Your God has caused this trouble. We will not have more of your God or your God-houses in this land."

"I'm sorry," Brentwood said. "But I swear before God Himself that no one here killed your brave. And this is our land too. Our God loves you and your people. We build our God-houses for you as well as for us. Just as your own Thayendanegea told you, God loves the Haudenosaunee just as much as He loves white people. Jesus is the Savior of everyone who believes."

"My son is dead," Thunder Arm said, as though Brentwood hadn't spoken a word. "You will pay with your blood."

Brentwood swayed and nearly fell. "Father," Paul said urgently. "You must have help! You're bleeding to death. Chip, tell Thunder Arm they can talk later."

Chip looked up at his father, and spoke rapidly, pointing to the arrows still sticking out of Brentwood's arm and thigh. But he might as well have been talking to a stone. Chip sighed. "Him not hear me," he said to Paul. "To him now I be dead like Black Hawk. More dead, because him still call Black Hawk fine brave."

Paul was horrified. "Please, Chief Thunder Arm," he pleaded. "I know you understand some English. Chip did this for us, because we're friends. He knows no one here killed—"

"You make vow to your God," Thunder Arm interrupted him. "You break vow. You show is not real God. We burn God-house. Kill God-man!" He pointed his arm at Brentwood.

"What's this about, Paul?" Brentwood asked quietly.

"I didn't break the vow!" Paul burst out, to both of them. "We didn't take the side of the white people. We just tried to stop the attack." He turned to his father. "The war council vowed to kill you. We had to stop it."

The settlers murmured among themselves, astonished.

Chip held his arm out to Thunder Arm, pleading, "Father, let the Redcoats find out who killed Black Hawk. These people are my friends."

For the first time Thunder Arm turned to Chip. He grasped his son's arm and held it up high. "What is this thing you have? Tell me. This is a symbol, Chipagawana."

223

Okot came forward, and he and Paul held out their wrists with the deerskin bands. "We are blood brothers," Chip told his father. "We have sworn this forever."

Black fury swept over Thunder Arm's stony face. "You have sworn? My first son is dead, and my last a traitor..."

"No!" Chip cried. "I am Onondaga. But these friends—they saved my life."

Brentwood stopped whatever Thunder Arm was going to say next by sagging on his feet and pitching headfirst into all of them.

"Enough of this!" Giant John shouted. He disentangled himself from Brentwood, letting another couple of the men lift the prostrate preacher and carry him to a bed of straw. Groping around in the air, he managed to grasp hold of the shaft of the arrow sticking into his shoulder. With a swift movement he yanked it out. One of the women, watching, swayed and fell over in a dead faint. John staggered a bit, and his face went a terrible shade of greeny gray. He whistled through his teeth, and said some things under his breath that Paul was sure weren't meant for anyone's ears. But Giant John smiled grimly as he broke the arrow over his knee, and he accepted a wide gingham kerchief from one of the women to press over his wound.

When he was breathing better, and the flow of blood had slowed again to a trickle, he turned back to face Thunder Arm. "You know me," he said in Onondaga. "I ate in your longhouse for one moon. I am a friend of the Onondaga." He turned and looked across the white faces to Swift Deer. "I saved your son's life."

Thunder Arm nodded. His eyes were narrowed into slits, but they kept flicking over to where Brentwood lay, as though to make certain his prey didn't get away.

"What about an exchange?" John said. "You want someone to pay for Black Hawk's murder. All right. I will." There was a gasp from those settlers who understood what he was saying, and a sudden stirring among the waiting warriors. "I didn't do it," John added. "I would never raise my arm against the Hotahyonhne clan of Thunder Arm. Swift Deer is my friend. I would myself kill the person who murdered his brother Black Hawk. I want you to be sure about that." He looked at the settlers gathered silently around them. "But God knows I've done enough to my own people that I deserve to die. If it will stop the bloodshed, then kill me instead of the preacher." His eyes flickered to Paul's pale face. "God knows too, that Brentwood is worth a hundred of me."

And, before the astonished settlers and Indians, Giant John, the toughest trapper in Upper Canada, dropped to his knees in front of Thunder Arm, with his hands over his head in full surrender.

"Mabior!" Okot breathed softly.

Thunder Arm turned to Eagle Wing. The other chief was allowed to approach him, and they consulted in whispers. After a few minutes Thunder Arm nodded, and summoned one of the waiting braves. The warrior handed him his quiver of arrows and his bow.

"No!" Brentwood had regained consciousness, and someone must have told him what was happening because he was struggling back to his feet. A nurse in the group had removed the arrows and was trying to bandage his wounds, but Brentwood waved her aside and stumbled back to Thunder Arm. "You can't do this! The Redcoats can find out and punish the murderer."

"Let it be, Brentwood," John said. "You're always preaching that one Man had to die for the sins of everyone else. So I guess I'm just following in the right footsteps. After all this time I guess that's a surprise to you."

"John..." Brentwood's voice broke. He put his hand on the trapper's shoulder.

Thunder Arm, barking an order to those around him, nocked an arrow on his bow and drew it back. Chip, Paul and Okot stood rooted to the ground, not daring to believe what was happening. Nothing disturbed the utter stillness.

The burst of commotion was like the first thunderclap in a quick violent storm. Swift Deer was struggling against the men holding him, snapping and snarling like a trapped wolf and shouting, "Let me go!" At least, that's what Chip told Paul and Okot afterwards. It sounded to them as though there must have been a lot more to it. But everyone had turned to look, even Giant John, and finally Swift Deer fought his way free. He plunged across the few yards like a drunkard, weaving and howling, holding his head as though it might explode. He flung himself at Thunder Arm's feet, shoving Giant John aside and grasping his father around the knees. "I can't let this happen," he said. "I can't let my friend die. I know who did it. I know who killed Black Hawk. Father, forgive my silence."

Once again the stillness in the clearing was electrifying. Giant John had picked himself up and was shaking his head as if to clear it.

When Swift Hawk spoke next, it was not in that anguished shout, but in a voice barely over a whisper. "It was an accident. We were hunting, and I pretended he was a bear on the trail. I had already shot the gun. I thought it was empty. I never used his gun before then. I didn't know it could happen. I was laughing, and so was he. I put the gun right up to his chest and pulled the trigger. And he fell over. Dead."

Of course, Paul and Okot didn't understand what Swift Deer had said. But his actions spoke more clearly than words. They watched Thunder Arm. The chief seemed to age before their eyes, as though time suddenly ran forward ten years, or twenty. He seemed to shrink and grow gray. After a minute, he stepped out of the circle of Swift Deer's arms, and walked away without looking back.

Storm was dying. He lay on his side with blood pooled in the dust all around him. Already his eyes were glazing over. When he breathed, it was like the noise of a little boy whacking a picket fence with a stick. Paul knelt beside him, cradling the horse's head on his lap. He thought about the night when they were attacked by the wolves, and for the first time since he was lost his eyes filled with tears.

Giant John crouched beside Paul and put an arm around his shoulder. "He's suffering, Paul. He's got a punctured lung and he's lost a lot of blood. He's suffocating."

Paul nodded without looking up. John left him, but was back in a minute with his rifle. Paul said, "Bye, fella," very softly. Then he got up and walked back to where his father lay.

BOOM!

The single shot echoed like a cannon blast around the clearing.

"Storm?" Brentwood asked.

Paul nodded. There was nothing else to say.

The war party had dispersed, the braves riding tiredly back to their own villages. All except Thunder Arm's band, which set up camp at the farthest end of the clearing from the buildings. Giant John, once his shoulder was bandaged by the nurse, organized a dray with another couple of men, and with Proudfoot and Raveneye pulling, they dragged away Storm's body.

The women among the settlers had rebuilt the campfires, and they heated water for washing, and for cleaning the many scrapes and cuts on Paul, Chip and Okot. Okot's bottom lip was cut and swollen, and one eye was puffy and bruised, but he hardly noticed those things. Like Paul and Chip, he was on pins and needles wondering what was going to happen. They were shy with the settlers—it felt so strange to be with other people again, after their weeks alone in the bush.

Sometime just after lunch, Thunder Arm approached the buildings by himself, and he disappeared into the house where Brentwood was lying on a straw mattress with his wounded leg propped up. Chip sat cross-legged with Paul and Okot by one of the fires, fiddling with his wristband and darting looks every few seconds at the cowhide that covered the doorway to the house. Paul bit his lip until it bled, and none of them spoke.

It seemed like hours before Thunder Arm reappeared. He walked back to his waiting braves with his eyes fixed straight ahead. Chip sighed. But almost immediately, someone whistled at Paul, and the boys were summoned into the house.

"Chipagawana," Brentwood said, "we thank you for what you have done today. You saved many lives. Thunder Arm has told me that he must disown you, because you have betrayed your people. But he also told me that he once hoped you would save your people from some great trouble, and this makes him even more hurt and disappointed." Brentwood closed his eyes for a moment, and the nurse slipped quietly up to him and wiped his face with a cool cloth.

Chip remembered the morning with the hunting party when he had shot the wild turkey, and Thunder Arm's words to the braves. Sadness washed over him like a cold stream.

Brentwood opened his eyes, and he smiled. "Chipagawana, I told him that he had spoken the truth about you. In stopping the massacre today, you saved Thunder Arm and all your clan from terrible punishment by the Redcoats. You can be quiet in your heart. Thunder Arm is still very unhappy. His first son is dead. His second has killed his own kin. He doesn't want to lose you. Tonight you will go to him, and you will be welcomed back to your longhouse and your mother's clan."

Paul and Okot clapped their stunned friend on the back, grinning happily. Brentwood then spoke to Paul. "For nearly two months I thought you were dead," he said. "Instead, God has brought you back strong and brave, almost a man. But it made me think things over, and we're going to change our lives. Another circuit preacher is on his way from England. I am going to be the pastor of this new church. This building is to be our house."

"A house of our own!" Paul exclaimed, looking around at the rough walls. "You mean, no more time on the trail?"

Brentwood laughed. "Don't look so upset. We'll still do a lot of visiting. But you're almost thirteen, and it's time you had some schooling. The building next to the church will be a school, and we've hired a teacher." He pointed to a couple of dusty crates in the corner. "That's schoolbooks. We had them shipped out from England."

Paul's face looked the way it had back in their clearing when Chip told him they were having raccoon for breakfast. "What if I don't want to go to school?" he demanded. "I'm too old. And I want to be a trapper. I've decided!" He looked defiantly at his father.

"Well, you can be a book-learned trapper," Brentwood said.

Okot tried not to snort with laughter. Chip muttered something under his breath in Onondaga, and Brentwood turned on him sternly. "Chipagawana, is this the kind of wicked influence you've had on my son?"

But Paul could see his father's lips were twitching. "What'd he say?" he asked suspiciously.

"He said it was too bad after all that he didn't let Thunder Arm burn down the buildings. All those books would have made a great bonfire."

And suddenly the tension was all gone. "One last thing," Brentwood said, turning to Okot. "I have heard a little of your story from Paul. You can tell me more when we are settled. But you must stay with us now. You and Paul can go to school together." He chuckled. "Then Paul won't be so worried about being the biggest in the class. Will you stay?"

Okot swallowed hard. He had a home, and friends…he had a place to learn to live with white men. He had everything…except his own family. He would never have that again. He tried to smile, and muttered, "Yes, thank you," to Brentwood.

Brentwood seemed to understand. "We'll pray for your family, for the others who are still slaves," he said. "Who knows what might happen? Our God can do great things."

Okot grinned. "Yes," he said. "I know. Mandy was right. She prayed for me to get here. And to see Jesus in my heart." He breathed a deep happy sigh.

"What will happen to Swift Deer?" Paul wondered aloud. "Will the Redcoats punish him?"

Brentwood shook his head. "That's for the Onondaga to sort out. But Thunder Arm is satisfied that it was an accident. I think Swift Deer and Giant John will go off trapping together for the winter. By springtime, feelings won't be running so hot, and his mother will welcome him home."

"Maybe Giant John stoled that French trapper's beaver pelts," Okot said. "Maybe that's why he thought he should make sacrifice."

"It's because he killed a man," Paul told him.

"Paul!" Brentwood said. "You know better than to repeat stories like that."

"Sorry," Paul muttered. But he soon brightened up. "Say, did you see Okot's stunt when he jumped Swift Deer? Standing on a horse's back? I told you, Okot, you're another Philip Astley."

"You was goin' to tell me this, and what's a circus too," Okot reminded him.

"He was a famous English rider who did great tricks like that," Paul explained. "He toured in Europe too, and started shows called circuses, to show these tricks to people."

"There's a circus in America too," Brentwood said. "Or there was, a few years ago."

"You mean, a man can live just by riding tricks on a horse?" Okot shook his head. "D'you think it's okay for a Christian?" he asked Brentwood uncertainly.

"About as okay as being a trapper, I suppose," Brentwood said. And he winked.

Towards sunset the three friends stood together on the edge of the great falls. All around them the mist made rainbows in the air, and the ground shook with the thunder of the mighty cataract. Just over the lip of the gorge, where they had hidden before the battle that morning, Chip's people waited for him to join them for the long ride back to Ohsweken. Chip was frowning. But Paul punched his friend in the arm. "We'll meet again soon," he said. "I have to come get my horse."

Thunder Arm had made a present of Raveneye to Okot, and he had promised Paul a horse too.

Chip untied something from his buckskin belt. "I make for you," he said. He took Paul's wrist with the friendship band, and quickly tied on a new one. This one was braided from long white hairs taken from Storm's mane. "To remember brave horse killed in battle."

Paul looked for a long time at the two braids. Finally he crossed his wrist over his friend's. "Thanks, Chip."

Chip nodded, and turned to walk away.

"See ya, Chipagawana!" Okot called after him.

Chip stopped. In a moment he came back to them. He pulled his knife from the sheath on his leg, and held it out to Okot. With his fingers he traced his name carved into the bone handle. "Keep it, Okot Deng." he said. "Finally you learn my name. Now you don't forget!"

He marched away, his twisted leg swinging out at every step, up the gorge to where his father was waiting. After a minute Okot pushed the sturdy hunting knife into his buckskin belt. Then he and Paul turned back to the camp and walked across the cleared land to their new home.

Glossary

Albino horse: a horse with a completely white coat, mane and tail, and unusual blue eyes.

Lead wolf, now known as Alpha Male: the lead male "in charge" of a wolf pack. Experts in wolf behavior can identify the alpha male by distinguishing characteristics such as the upright angle at which it carries its tail.

Bannock: thick cornbread.

Bloodroot: a plant known as Red Puccoon (*Sanguinaria canadensis*), called bloodroot because of its red root and red root *sap*.

Brave: a young North American Native man who has proved himself as a warrior on the *warpath*.

Clearing: an open area in the middle of woods or a forest where young trees and plants take root in the ground layer of decaying leaves or coniferous needles.

Cobra: the common name for many species of a poisonous snake native to Africa, southern Asia and the Philippines. Cobra venom contains a deadly toxin that acts on the nervous system. The king cobra is the longest poisonous snake in the world, growing up to 18 feet (5.5 m) in length. The spitting cobra blinds its prey by spraying venom into the eyes from as far away as 8 feet (1.4 m). The common cobra is the snake most often used by snake charmers.

Copse: a thicket of small trees.

Dinka: extraordinarily tall, slender black people, noted for their exceptional strength and endurance, native to what is now the Republic of the Sudan in central Africa. Known to themselves as Monyjang, the Dinka have lived in the area of the White Nile, a tributary of the Nile River, since the tenth century, where they raise cattle, sheep and goats. Wealth is measured in cattle, and the Dinka will fight or kill to defend their own. Cattle provide everything essential to their existence: dung for fuel, dairy products, which are the staple of their diet, hides for bedding, and horns for various implements. Cattle are sacrificed to appease enemies, spirits, and ancestors, killed for special feasts, given as a dowry when a woman is married, and as compensation for all kinds of crimes, including murder. See *Mabior*.

Dray: a strong low cart, without sides and often without wheels, used to drag heavy loads.

Dream fast: a test of strength and endurance through which *Iroquois* (*Haudenosaunee*) boys became men of their tribe. A boy of about fourteen years spent several days and nights by himself in a sacred wilderness place, fasting and praying for the Great Spirit to show him the animal or bird that would be his guardian for the rest of his life.

Factor: the man in charge of looking after slaves during the time that the slave merchants negotiated their sale. Factors paid for the slaves' food, in return for which they received a percentage of the sale price.

Flint: hard quartz that produces a spark when struck against steel. Before the invention of matches, flint and steel was the easiest way of lighting a fire. In the seventeenth and eighteenth centuries, flint was used in guns called "flintlocks" to strike a spark that would ignite the gunpowder.

Gibbous moon: the phase when more than half but less than the full moon is illuminated. The name comes from the Latin word *gibbus*, which means "hump," because the moon looks as though it has a hump on one side.

Glade: an open space like a field or meadow that is surrounded by woods.

Gunwale (pronounced "gunnel"): the upper edge (rising above the deck) of the sides on a boat.

Hackamore: a plaited bridle, made of horsehair or rawhide, used in western-style horsemanship, that does not have a bit for the horse's mouth.

Haudenosaunee (pronounced "hoo-dee-noh-SHAW-nee"): the *Iroquois* name for their own tribe, meaning "people of the *longhouse*."

Hotahyonhne: *Iroquois* (*Haudenosaunee*) word meaning "wolf."

Hobble: a strap, piece of rope, or shackles similar to handcuffs, used to fasten the legs of a horse (usually the forelegs) to keep it from straying.

Iroquois: several North American Indian tribes speaking similar languages. These included the *Onondaga* (Chipagawana's people), Huron and Mohawk tribes. The Iroquois lived in villages surrounded by *palisades*. They grew crops, including corn, squash, beans and tobacco. The men fished and hunted, traveled and traded, defended the village, and went on the *warpath*.

Juur: *Dinka* word meaning foreigners.

Longhouse: a communal building where related families of an *Iroquois* (*Haudenosaunee*) tribe lived. The longhouse family is matriarchal (based on the female, rather than the male, line of descent) and is the basic unit of Iroquois society. Longhouses were built from evergreen poles covered with sheets of elm bark.

Mabior: the name given to the white bull sacrificed by the *Dinka* people to appease the spirits, or for atonement, when someone has committed a crime.

Matchenawtowaig: the Ottawa tribe's name for themselves.

Methodist circuit preacher: a traveling preacher under the direction of the Methodist Missionary Society. Usually unmarried, these circuit preachers lived tough and lonely lives, traveling on horseback in circuits that took about six weeks to complete. They rode in all weathers, and faced danger from Indians, hecklers among their own people, and the elements, which put many of them in an early grave. When the weather was really bad, it was often said to be "good for no one except a circuit rider."

Monyjang: the *Dinka* word for their own people; it means "The Man of Men." This means that they consider themselves as the best measure of man's dignity, and that everyone else (*juur*: foreigners) is inferior.

Nock: to "nock" an arrow means to fit it onto the bowstring ready to shoot. "Nock" is also a noun referring to the notch or groove at the end of an arrow into which the bowstring fits.

Onondaga: one of the six nations making up the *Iroquois* (*Haudenosaunee*) tribes. The name means "people of the hills." The Onondaga sided with the British during the American Revolution. After the war, most of this tribe settled in a reservation on the Grand River, in the southern part of the Canadian province of Ontario. Many of their descendents still live in that region.

Overseer: a man in charge of directing and disciplining the slaves on a *plantation*. Overseers had great power over slaves, since the law considered slaves as articles of property, with no rights as human beings. Slaves could be whipped, starved, mutilated, tortured, or even killed, at the hands of an overseer, or at his orders.

Palisade: a fence made of sturdy pointed wooden poles driven into the ground, built as a defensive enclosure around forts and Indian villages.

Paint (pinto): a horse with a dappled or mottled coat, usually black and white, and sometimes including brown.

Pemmican: a staple food of North American Indians, fur trappers, traders and even early settlers. Dried deer, moose, caribou or buffalo meat was ground to a powder between two stones, and then mixed with animal fat and occasionally dried berries. Stored in pouches made from hide, this high-energy survival food was easy to carry on the trail and lasted for months.

Pitch: a black or dark sticky substance produced by evergreen trees. It was smeared on elm-bark and birch-bark canoes to make them waterproof. Noah's ark was sealed with pitch.

Plantation: a working farm or estate in a tropical or subtropical area, where crops such as tobacco, cotton, sugar beets and coffee are grown; usually with laborers who live on the estate in dwellings provided by the owner. From the earliest days of colonization in America, black African slaves were imported to work on plantations.

Resin: a yellowish-brown sticky substance produced by evergreen trees. Lumps of resin burn easily and are good for starting fires. In the past resin was used to seal jars, and as a medicine.

Rowan: the mountain ash tree, which has clumps of vivid orange berries in the fall.

Sap: a watery liquid, usually clear, that circulates nutrients through plants and trees just as blood does in people and animals. Sap contains a lot of sugar. Sap from maple trees is boiled down to produce maple syrup and maple sugar candy.

Savannah: African grasslands

Skewer: a pin or stick made of metal or wood, used to hold meat together while it is roasting.

Slave trade: millions of black Africans were shipped by European slavers from the 1500s to the 1800s, to what are now Latin America and the United States. Most came from the Western Sudan, an area of Africa extending from the Sahara desert in the north to the Gulf of Guinea in the south, and from Lake Chad in the east all the way across to the Atlantic Ocean. Slavery had been practiced in Africa for centuries, and many Africans were sold to European slavers by their own people, by hostile tribes, or by Arabs. Slaves in the American colonies were usually field laborers on *plantations*. Others were used as household servants, stable hands, and farm workers. Slavery was a highly controversial practice that led in part to the American Civil War (1861–1865). The first three presidents of the States were against slavery. In 1778, Thomas Jefferson (third president) was responsible for the passage of a bill that, at least officially, outlawed the importation of slaves into Virginia. Slavery was abolished in *Upper Canada* in 1793. After the War of 1812, many runaway slaves arrived in Upper Canada from the United States, and settled in the southwest area around Chatham, Windsor and especially Amherstburg, on Lake Erie. In Britain William Wilberforce, a Member of Parliament and an evangelical Christian, lobbied most of his life for an end to the slave trade. Britain abolished slavery in 1833, one month after Wilberforce's death, giving freedom to all slaves throughout the British Empire.

Staring coat: a term used to describe the hair of a mammal, especially a horse, that has a dull appearance and coarse feel due to illness, injury or malnutrition.

Tack: stable gear used on a riding horse, such as the saddle and bridle.

Thayendanegea (Joseph Brant), 1742–1807: A Mohawk Indian chief who was converted to Christianity and served as a missionary among his own people. He translated parts of the New Testament into the Mohawk language. Brant aided the British in the French and Indian War, and fought against the Americans in the American Revolution. In 1774, he was made Secretary to the British Superintendent of Indian Affairs. He traveled to England in 1775, and again in 1785, when he helped raise funds to build the first Episcopal church in *Upper Canada*, in what is now Brantford, Ontario.

Tinder: any dry material, such as twigs, cotton, dead leaves and conifer cones, that easily catches fire from a spark. The word was originally used for anything used for catching the spark off a flint and steel for fire, or lighting a candle or oil lamp.

Trading post: the place where a company or independent traders traded local products, such as furs, in areas where there were few, or widely-scattered, settlements.

Upper Canada: the southern part of the Canadian province of Ontario that was a British province from 1791–1840.

Warpath: a route taken by North American Indians intending to start or join in a war with neighboring or enemy tribes. Warfare was an important aspect of *Iroquois* (*Haudenosaunee*) society. Young men earned respect and honor in their tribes by showing their bravery on the warpath.

Withers: the high ridge between the shoulder bones of a horse, at the base of the neck.

Wolverine: also called a "devil bear" or "woods devil," the wolverine is a relative of the mink and weasel. The fur is highly valued because of its durability, and because the guard hairs resist frost accumulation. Wolverines are not good hunters, but will eat almost anything they can find or kill. They have powerful jaws that can crush bones and frozen meat. Wolverines often robbed the traps of fur traders, tearing apart and eating the trapped and helpless animals.

Zorilla: a large rodent native to central and south Africa, very much like a skunk.

Notes

_____

_____

_____

_____

_____

_____

_____

_____

_____

_____

_____

_____

_____

_____

_____

_____

Notes

Notes

Notes

Notes

Notes

Notes

Notes

_____

_____

_____

_____

_____

_____

_____

_____

_____

_____

_____

_____

_____

_____

_____

Notes

Notes

Notes

Notes

_____

_____

_____

_____

_____

_____

_____

_____

_____

_____

_____

_____

_____

_____

_____